'Rank gets y
Sister Clark.

'Thanks for the warning, Nathan —
'And here was I thinking that after years of work I would finally be assured of fawning consideration from the lowly masses.'

'Ha! You obviously haven't heard the one nurses tell about consultants being like monkeys—the higher up the tree they climb, the more you see of their less attractive aspects!'

There were several seconds of stunned silence before a husky chuckle turned into full-throated laughter. And Karen suddenly realised that this man was a member of those upper echelons!

Josie Metcalfe lives in Cornwall now with her long-suffering husband, four children and two horses, but, as an Army brat frequently on the move, books became the only friends who came with her wherever she went. Now that she writes them herself she is making new friends, and hates saying goodbye at the end of a book—but there are always more characters in her head clamouring for attention until she can't wait to tell their stories.

Recent titles by the same author:

FOR NOW, FOR ALWAYS
WORTH WAITING FOR
LOUD AND CLEAR
FORGOTTEN PAIN
BOUND BY HONOUR
A VOICE IN THE DARK

A WISH
FOR CHRISTMAS

BY
JOSIE METCALFE

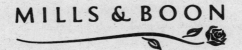

MILLS & BOON

*MILLS & BOON, the Rose Device and
LOVE ON CALL are trademarks of the publisher.
Harlequin Mills & Boon Limited,
Eton House, 18-24 Paradise Road, Richmond, Surrey TW9 1SR*

© Josie Metcalfe 1996

ISBN 0 263 79998 0

*Set in Times 10 on 12 pt. by
Rowland Phototypesetting Limited
Bury St Edmunds, Suffolk*

03-9612-46796

Made and printed in Great Britain

AUTHOR'S NOTE

MAKE-A-WISH is a foundation with a simple purpose—
to try to grant the favourite wishes of children suffering
from life-threatening illnesses.

With the help of fund-raisers and donations large and
small they are able to provide treasured memories for
all the family when, perhaps, time finally runs out. . .
Memories that are in total contrast to their accustomed
routine of hospitals, doctors and treatment.

Sometimes, granting a wish can be the miracle that
takes the hurt away for a while, whether it's meeting a
favourite pop or sports star, being a bridesmaid or even
travelling to Lapland to meet Father Christmas. . .

CHAPTER ONE

'ARE you married?'

Matthew Beckett's clear, childish treble drew Karen's attention towards his serious little face. Her hands stilled about their task, the thermometer forgotten.

'No.' She smiled to hide the dull twist deep inside at this reminder of what might have been. 'I'm not married,' she confirmed as her eyes dropped to inspect the thread of mercury and she recorded her findings on the chart.

'Why not?' The question followed her, the persistence typical of a six-year-old boy unaltered by the severity of his illness. 'Don't you like children?'

'Of course I do. That's why I work in the hospital— so I can help look after them.'

'But you haven't got any of your own?' he demanded.

'I've got a whole wardful,' Karen replied lightly, her throat aching as Matthew's single-mindedness stirred up the shadows of lost dreams she'd thought she'd finally managed to banish in the last six months.

'But when you go home. . .aren't you sad that you haven't got some of your own?' His deep blue eyes gazed up at her so seriously. 'If you had a daddy, you could make some.'

'Ah.' Karen smiled her comprehension and perched on the edge of the bed. The light over his bed cast a wedge of brightness over his slight frame and she found her hand reaching naturally to smooth the thick thatch of dark blond hair away from his pale forehead. 'The trouble is, I've been wishing for a handsome prince to come along and he hasn't arrived yet.'

'A prince?' She watched as his expression grew intrigued at the thought. 'You want to marry a prince like the one in the Walt Disney films?'

'He wouldn't have to be exactly the same,' she conceded, hiding a smile as she recognised the boyish horror of anything romantic.

'What *will* he look like, then?' he challenged.

'Oh. Let me see.' Karen pretended to give it some consideration. 'I think he'll have to be a bit taller than you are, won't he?'

Matthew giggled, the solemn look banished from his face by her teasing.

'But I think he could have the same colour hair as yours, and definitely the same colour eyes—I've always loved that deep sapphire-blue. . .' Her voice trailed away as she realised that she'd lost his attention to something behind her.

'Daddy!' His little face lit up in welcome. 'Karen's going to marry a handsome prince with eyes the same colour as mine.'

Karen slid to her feet and turned to face the man who'd joined her beside the hospital bed, looking up a good eight inches into a pair of the most beautiful dark blue eyes she'd ever seen.

Under his cool gaze she was suddenly aware of herself as a woman for the first time in six months. Under his cool gaze she was very conscious that she was looking far from her best, with her uniform wilted at the end of a long shift, her nose shiny and her hair less than immaculate, and she felt a slight flush of heat climb into her cheeks.

'Staff Nurse.' He nodded a brief acknowledgement, the effect of the slightly husky tone of his voice on her nerve-endings reminding her of the stroke of a cat's tongue, before he turned away to greet his son.

Karen stepped aside silently to allow him to take her place at Matthew's side, feeling unaccountably dismissed when he turned his back on her to settle one hip in exactly the same place as her own had been.

For a moment she stood watching as he leant towards his son, the light gleaming over two heads of identical dark blond hair as he gave his son a gentle hug, and although his husky murmur was indecipherable to Karen she saw the whole-hearted smile it brought to Matthew's face.

Suddenly Karen felt as though she was intruding on something very private between the two of them, and when he straightened so that the slight figure in the bed was completely hidden behind the breadth of his father's shoulders she slipped quietly away.

She was just getting ready to go off duty and dreading the journey home in the damp chill of the dark winter evening when she heard the husky rasp of his voice again.

'Could I have a moment, Staff Nurse?' he said quietly over her shoulder, and she couldn't help stiffening against the reaction which rippled over her skin as she turned towards him in the hush of the empty corridor.

'How can I help you, Mr Beckett?' She kept her voice light and pleasant by dint of burying her hands in her deep coat pockets and clenching them into fists. What on earth was the matter with her? It must be sheer tiredness which was making her react so strangely to him.

'I wanted to talk to you about my son, Matthew,' he

began, gesturing with one hand for her to precede him through the door beside them and into the empty day room beyond.

'In that case, you need to speak to his doctor or to Sister Clark. I'm only a staff nurse and probably won't be able to—'

'It was Sister Clark who suggested I spoke to you,' he interrupted. 'She said you seemed to have formed a bond with Matthew almost as soon as he arrived on the ward this morning.'

Karen couldn't help smiling.

'He's a delightful child. You and your wife must be very proud of the way he's coping with his illness.'

'I'm not married.' There was the crackle of frost in his voice and his face was stony.

'I'm sorry,' she murmured, feeling chilled by the waves of disapproval he radiated. 'I didn't know. . .'

'The information is in Matthew's case-notes,' he said shortly, fixing her with a fierce gaze. 'I'd be grateful if you'd make sure the rest of the staff know so they don't mention her. I won't have Matthew upset by people reminding him that his mother walked out on him when he became ill.'

Karen couldn't help the sharp gasp of horror which escaped her at the blunt words.

'Surely she couldn't have known. . .' she began.

'Ha!' The brief bark could hardly be called laughter. 'Don't waste your time trying to make excuses for her. She made quite certain that Matthew understood exactly why she was leaving him by telling him to his face.'

'My God,' Karen breathed, unable to comprehend such cruelty towards a child. 'How *could* she?'

'Quite easily, apparently. Especially when he failed to come up to her expectations of perfection.' He stopped speaking suddenly as though horrified to realise just how much he had revealed.

'Anyway,' he continued, 'that wasn't why I wanted to speak to you. I wanted to know how you think he's coping with the move.'

'Well, it's a little early to tell,' she temporised. 'He only arrived this morning and so far all his observations have been within the figures at his previous hospital. I don't see why his treatment shouldn't—'

'I'm sorry,' he interrupted her again. 'Obviously I didn't make myself clear. I know all I need to about his medical situation; what I want to know from you is how he has settled in emotionally.'

For a moment Karen was taken aback. It was the first time she had been asked such a question in just that way and didn't quite know how to reply.

'Sister Clark did say you were with him when he had the latest tests done and that you spent some time with him this afternoon,' he prompted.

'He's an amazing little boy,' she murmured after a brief pause to collect her thoughts. 'One minute he's just a typical six-year-old wanting to watch cartoons on the television and the next he's talking quite seriously about the possibility of finding a bone marrow donor in time.'

As she watched, a wintry smile briefly touched the corners of his mouth then faded away.

'Yes,' he murmured. 'He is amazing. To have gone through so much. . .'

'*He* told *me* that he's due to start another course of chemotherapy this week,' she volunteered.

'Yes. We're still trying to get him into remission.' There was genuine pain in his voice in spite of the tight rein he had on his emotions and Karen had the feeling that he didn't dare let them loose in case he completely fell apart—not that he gave the impression of being a man who would admit it.

'From what I can remember of his notes, they're trying a slightly different cocktail of drugs this time, so perhaps this combination will work better for him. He's struck me as being a real little fighter and given half a chance. . .' It was so difficult to know what to say. She desperately wanted to be able to reassure him that his beautiful son would beat the leukaemia which was destroying his life but her conscience would never allow her to give him false hope just in case. . .

'Last time he only complained once.' The husky voice broke into the silence surrounding them and Karen found her eyes drawn to the lines of strain etched around his mouth as he continued. 'He was being terribly sick and his mouth was full of ulcers but the only thing he complained about was losing his hair.' He pressed his lips tightly together and she heard him draw in a deep breath.

Out of the corner of her eye she saw the rhythmic flex and release as he clenched his hands into fists then unclenched them, and her natural compassion forced her to reach out swiftly to grasp one tautly muscled arm.

'We'll be doing everything we can,' she said earnestly, somehow knowing deep inside that he needed the physical contact, no matter how fleeting. 'If this combination makes his hair fall out, I'll make sure I remind him that it'll grow back again.'

For several seconds he seemed stunned, his deep blue eyes holding hers as though he wanted to see right inside her head before they dropped to where her slender fingers lay forgotten against the dark fabric of his sleeve.

'Well,' Karen muttered in embarrassment as she snatched her hand away and tucked it back into her pocket. 'I suppose I'd better. . .'

'Please.' The husky plea stopped her hurried flight and her eyes were drawn inexorably back to his own, so filled with pain. 'I. . . He's all I've got and. . . Thank you. Thank you for caring about him.'

'That's part of what nursing is all about—caring,' she said through a throat tight with emotion.

'It's more than that,' he said positively. 'Every doctor and nurse cares about their patients, otherwise they would never stand the setbacks in the job, but this is something more than that.'

'You could be right,' Karen admitted with a wry smile. 'Perhaps I just happen to be a pushover for little fighters like Matthew.'

'Ah, yes.' For the first time she saw the smile reach his eyes. 'You told Matthew you were looking for a blond prince with sapphire-blue eyes.'

For a second she was breathless as his own dark eyes, so much like his son's, gleamed down into hers and a deep quiver of response startled her as it flashed through her like lightning.

'That's right.' Her own smile was slow in coming. 'All I have to do now is cross my fingers for him and wait for him to grow up.'

'Coming,' Karen managed through a yawn, raising her hand in acknowledgement to Sister Clark as she turned to stuff the last of her belongings into the small remaining space in her locker. It felt as though she'd never left the place last night, let alone gone home to sleep. Sometimes she felt as though she never quite caught up with herself.

'Here.' Valerie Clark held out a thick white mug emblazoned with the motto 'Caution. Work in progress.' 'You look as if you could do with this.'

'Thanks.' Karen took a sip of the steaming brew before she sank into a chair beside the desk piled high with papers and files, the amount hardly changed in spite of the introduction of computerisation. 'You're a life-saver.' She took another mouthful. 'Right. What's the bad news? I don't usually get welcomed with coffee.'

'It's a domino day,' Valerie said cryptically, knowing that Karen would understand what she meant.

'Already!' she groaned. 'What started them all toppling this time?'

'Mark Hooper's parents were involved in an accident last night.'

'Damn,' Karen muttered forcefully. 'As if they haven't got enough on their plates. How badly were they hurt? Was Mark injured too?' She'd had a soft spot for the youngster ever since the first time he'd come on the ward. He was another gallant little fighter, like Matthew Beckett.

'Mark was badly shaken but otherwise unharmed. Unfortunately, his parents weren't so lucky so he's going to have to come in to us for a while until they're fit enough to take him home. Obviously it's not the ideal situation for him, but Social Services can't come up with a temporary home with someone willing to be responsible for his medical needs.'

'He hasn't got any other family to take him, has he?' She frowned as she tried to remember.

'No. Only an elderly set of grandparents who wouldn't be able to cope—apparently they were on their way back from visiting when another car jumped the lights.'

'And I bet *he* just walked away from the mayhem he'd caused without a scratch,' Karen said in a resigned tone.

'More or less,' Valerie agreed. 'They say the devil looks after his own. . .' She up-ended her own mug to reveal the motto 'Time for another one' emblazoned on the bottom and made Karen chuckle as she drained her own.

'When is Mark due and how long do they reckon his parents will be here?' she queried, getting down to details.

'He's already arrived. I was just settling him in the day room when Matthew Beckett appeared and offered to keep him company.' She shook her head. 'He's so adult for a six-year-old. Mark's seven but Matthew was as protective towards him as if *he* was the elder one.'

Karen was filled with a strange glow of pride and had to give herself a mental shake to remind herself that she had no right to feel that way about Matthew, even if he did seem to have tied a string around her heart.

'Would it be a good idea to put them in adjacent beds?' she suggested. 'Mark's an old hand in the ward so he could take Matthew under his wing while it's all so strange to him.'

'And Matthew can return the favour with Mark until he recovers from the shock of the accident,' Valerie finished. 'Good idea. Let's get it organised. The sooner Mark gets into the routine of things, the sooner he'll regain a sense of security.'

They had finished settling the two lads into their new quarters and were busily getting on with the routine work of a busy specialist children's ward when Valerie took yet another phone call.

'Karen?' She appeared at the door to her office looking rather flustered and beckoned her over. 'That was Jenny Barber up on Surgical with a two-minute warning that the new oncologist is on his way down to us. He's—'

The sound of the ward doors opening cut her words off and Karen turned in time to see Matthew's father enter and stride towards them.

'Hello.' She smiled a little tentatively as she found his eyes fixed squarely on her and her heart gave an extra beat. 'We've given Matthew a change of scenery and a new neighbour since you were here last night.'

'Staff Nurse.' He nodded an acknowledgement then flicked his gaze across to Valerie to repeat it. 'Sister. I'm sorry to descend on you at such short notice.'

Karen frowned as she tried to decipher the meaning of his words and the strange change in his manner, and it wasn't until she saw that the small group of people who had followed him into the ward were also following him into Valerie's office that the penny suddenly dropped.

'Unfortunately—' he turned and propped his hip on the edge of her desk as he continued speaking to Valerie even as Karen tried to sort out the scrambled pieces of information in her head '—Mr Firzal had a stroke last night so the hospital management committee have asked me to step in straight away.'

'Oh, no,' Karen murmured, genuinely upset to hear that the consultant oncologist had been taken ill. 'How is he?'

'Under observation at the moment, of course, but it looks as if it was just a minor one.'

'Will he be coming back to us when he's recovered?' Valerie asked, sharing Karen's liking for the quietly spoken man. 'The children all love him.'

'It's unlikely,' one of the faceless, grey-suited administrators interjected from his position behind Matthew's father. 'Mr Firzal had been thinking about cutting down to part-time work for some time and this has made him decide to relinquish the reins to Mr Beckett straight away.'

Karen was still reeling at the revelation that Matthew Beckett's father was their new consultant.

As he was the parent of one of their young patients she had been expecting to see quite a bit of him until Matthew either recovered or they lost him to the ravages of the leukaemia; now, in his capacity as the new consultant oncologist, she could look forward to seeing him on a regular basis for years. . .

'I'm afraid I'm going to rely fairly heavily on you and your staff for the next few weeks, Sister.' The husky voice broke into her rambling thoughts. 'I wasn't supposed to start work until the beginning of January, to give me time to move house and see my son through his next course of chemotherapy. . .'

He threw a glance towards the window which overlooked the ward and Karen watched a strained smile lighten his expression when he saw his son concentrating fiercely on the game he was playing with his new companion.

Turning back towards them, he continued. 'This means that I haven't had a chance to spend any time shadowing Saleh either here or up on the surgical ward. I'm going to need you to give me a shout or push me in the right direction until I find my feet.'

Even the sober-suited administrator smiled at the

thought of any of the nurses having the temerity to push the awe-inspiring Mr Beckett around, then glanced at his watch and commented that if he'd finished visiting the various wards there was still a great deal of paperwork for them to complete in his office.

'Paperwork!' Valerie snorted when the door finally clicked shut behind the last of them. 'I swear you could bury this hospital in the amount of paperwork we have to get through in a year.'

Karen groaned in agreement, her thoughts still full of the way the rest of the group had been forced to wait impatiently when Mr Beckett had insisted on spending a few minutes with his son.

For the first time she had been in a position to see the changes wrought in him by a genuine smile as he listened to Mark and Matthew chattering at full speed about the game they were playing.

'I never connected Matthew's name with the new consultant,' Valerie mused when they'd finished the midday drugs round and were taking advantage of a momentary lull to grab a mug of coffee. 'I must have been on a day off when he visited before. Do you remember him?'

'I don't think so.' Karen screwed up her forehead as she thought. 'He didn't look familiar.'

'Oh, come on!' Valerie chided. 'You can't tell me you'd have forgotten him in a hurry. He's gorgeous!'

'Valerie! What would Tom say if he could hear you?'

'I'm married, not dead,' she pointed out swiftly. 'As long as I'm only looking, it proves my hormones are still fighting fit, so Tom should be delighted!'

Karen joined in her laughter but wondered at her own strange response to the man. Had Gareth's cruelty had a permanent effect on her or would she eventually be able to look at a handsome man and appreciate his charms the way Valerie did?

She gave a silent sigh and shook her head. As she had absolutely no intention of going through that sort of pain again, she wouldn't be allowing any man to get close enough for it to matter, whether he was a gargoyle or an Adonis.

'Do you think he intends keeping to all Mr Firzal's operating timetables?' she ventured, determined to keep her mind on work. 'We were expecting that little boy with the Wilms' tumour to come in tomorrow to prepare for surgery.'

Valerie blinked. 'I've no idea,' she admitted. 'I'd better make some phone calls to find out, in case it's one of the things he said we'd need to shout about.'

Karen spent the rest of her shift shadowed by a student nurse who was thinking about qualifying as a Registered Sick Children's Nurse and took every opportunity to grill her mentor about her experiences on the RSCN course.

'So, you've done your first year and you've definitely decided you want to specialise in nursing children?'

'Yes,' Holly Burton declared quietly with a slight lift to her determined chin. 'Eventually, I hope to make sister and have responsibility for a ward of my own, so I want to make sure I get all the relevant qualifications.'

Her earnestness made Karen want to smile. How long ago it seemed since she was that young and fresh-faced about life.

'Well, once you get to staff nurse, if you're an RSCN you'll have a deeper specialist knowledge and you'll be able to take on a greater degree of responsibility.'

'How hard is it? Not that I'm looking for an easy

ride,' she added quickly in case Karen had misunderstood. 'I just want to know what it'll involve.'

'You'll certainly have to spend a fair amount of your free time with your nose buried in books,' Karen warned. 'It's the only way to make sure you know the work before you're faced with it on the ward.'

'But you would recommend that I do it—as I'm intending to specialise in paediatric nursing?'

'As far as I'm concerned, I think it should be compulsory for every paediatric nurse,' Karen replied firmly. 'Nursing has progressed so much this century and technology is dragging it even further. The only way we can keep pace is to make sure we produce better and better qualified nurses.'

'I've heard that in some branches of medicine the nurses' qualifications are even higher than those of the doctors who give out the orders.' There was a wicked glint in Holly's eye as she offered the suggestion, and Karen responded with a sly wink.

'*You* know that and *I* know it,' she murmured out of the side of her mouth like a character in a bad spy film. 'But if we keep it to ourselves and just get on with the job it will help to preserve the doctors' fragile egos until they can take the shock!'

Their shared laughter set the tone for the rest of the day, with the two of them working companionably together. Karen had always enjoyed the teaching role involved in working with the junior nurses and she found it a pleasure to instruct someone as keen to learn as Holly. She only needed to have a procedure explained once before she had grasped the reasons for the methodology and her natural manual dexterity made techniques seem easy.

'She's got a good manner with the children, too,'

Karen reported to Valerie just before hand-over at the end of their shift. 'One or two of the parents seemed a little bemused by how young she looked but she soon managed to set them straight without getting anyone's back up.'

'She only looks so young because she's surrounded by old crocks like us,' Valerie said with a grimace. 'Just because we didn't go straight from school into nursing.'

'Ah, but we brought with us the skills afforded by our greater maturity,' Karen hammed in a pompous-sounding voice, and they both chuckled.

'You never did tell me what you were doing before you started your nursing training,' Valerie commented. 'I told you about my dreadful teenage marriage and my better luck second time around with Tom, but you're still a dark horse.'

'I took care of my parents,' Karen admitted softly, restricting herself to the simplest of explanations. 'They were almost housebound for several years, and once Father went Mother didn't last long.'

'I'm sorry.' Valerie's hand covered one of hers in an expression of sympathy. 'Were you the only daughter?'

'Only daughter, only child, and they were very old-fashioned in many ways. They wouldn't have a stranger coming into the house to take care of them. They believed that it was their right to have me throw up my career just to fetch and carry for them.'

Karen was glad that the staff coming on duty arrived then so that Valerie couldn't pursue the topic, knowing that a hint of the old bitterness had begun to creep into her voice.

Although she felt that she had largely come to terms with the events of the last few years, she didn't yet feel comfortable talking about them to other people. As far as her colleagues were concerned, she had come into nursing late and had become a dedicated career-woman.

The next morning Mark's mood had changed drastically and in spite of everyone's best efforts he didn't want to talk.

Valerie was even contemplating sending for one of the consultants in case it was a delayed result of the car crash or a sudden worsening of his condition, when suddenly Karen had an idea.

'Give me a few minutes,' she murmured as she noticed the similar expression on Matthew's face. 'I've got a feeling that someone else already knows what's the matter with Mark. All I've got to do is find a way to get him to tell me.'

Karen was impressed with Matthew's loyalty towards his new friend, but once he realised that everyone was worried that Mark was feeling ill he finally decided to tell Karen about it.

'It's about his wish,' he whispered, as if Mark could hear him all the way from the day room where Karen had taken him.

'His wish?' Karen queried, hearing the stress Matthew was putting on the important word but without understanding.

'Yes.' He nodded fervently. 'Some Wish people were going to take Mark and his mum and dad to see the real Father Christmas, but now they're all in hospital he won't be able to go because it's nearly Christmas and they're too ill.'

At last the penny dropped. Karen could hardly have spent the last year involved with such seriously ill children without hearing about Make-A-Wish and the miracles they tried to perform for her young charges.

'Did he tell you whether Sister knows about his wish?' she questioned gently.

'She's the one who told the Wish people about it,' he replied earnestly. 'They came to his house and talked to him about his three best wishes in the whole world and then they said he was going on a plane to see Father Christmas and his reindeer and. . .and everything.'

Two fat tears spilled over his lower lids and rolled down his pale cheeks to leave broad, silvery trails.

'Oh, Matthew. Don't upset yourself.' She curved one arm around his shoulders and gave him a gentle squeeze. 'Now that I know what's the matter with Mark, I can start to find out what we can do about it.'

'Do you think the Wish people will be able to make his mum and dad well in time to go?'

The open expression of hope on his face made Karen feel like crying herself.

'No, sweetheart. They can't do those sort of wishes. But I promise I'll go straight to Sister and get her to telephone the Wish people and tell them what's happened. If you go back to Mark and tell him to cross his fingers and make a really big wish, we'll see what we can do.'

Like the sun coming out after a shower, his smile eclipsed the misery which had filled him on his friend's behalf and he barely paused at the doorway to gasp a hurried, 'Thank you,' before he was on his way back to Mark.

'If only everything could be solved with crossed fingers and a really big wish,' a familiar husky voice said, and Matthew's father stepped into view in the doorway.

Karen's heart stuttered for several beats and she

firmly dismissed the crazy feeling as the result of surprise.

'It would certainly make our jobs a lot easier,' she commented wryly as she pushed herself up out of the squashy settee and straightened her uniform.

'I heard enough to gather that we've got a major problem on our hands with Mark,' he said as he stepped forward to perch on the arm of the matching chair.

'It certainly won't do much for his morale, or Matthew's, if this trip has to be cancelled,' she agreed. 'It's not as if it's the sort of wish that can be granted at any other time of year.'

'And going by his medical notes it's extremely unlikely that Mark will still be around to go next year instead,' he said, then sighed heavily as he stood up again. 'I suppose all we can do now is get Sister Clark to contact them. If she tells them what's happened to Mark's parents and throws the ball into their court perhaps they can come up with a solution.'

CHAPTER TWO

KAREN couldn't wait to get to the hospital the next day.

She'd hated going home at the end of her shift without knowing whether a solution had been found to Mark's misery, and her first stop as soon as she'd shed her heavy winter coat was Sister's office.

'Well?' she demanded eagerly. 'Have they managed to work it out?'

'And a good morning to you too,' Valerie teased over her shoulder as she poured milk into a mug and stirred.

'Sorry!' Karen pulled a wry face as she raised both palms in a gesture of peace. 'Good morning, Sister Clark. I do hope you slept well last night and had a good journey to work this morning. Now, what about Mark's trip?'

'Here, grab this and sit down.' Valerie was laughing as she turned to hold the brimming mug out to her friend. 'I don't think I've ever known anyone so single-minded as you are when you get your teeth into something.'

'Val!' Karen wrapped both hands around the mug to warm her hands up after the chilly walk into the hospital, but thought darkly about wrapping them around her superior's neck instead.

'All right! Keep your hair on!' she soothed, and Karen watched impatiently as she propped herself against the edge of her desk. 'I managed to get hold of one of the members of the regional team in charge of organising Mark's wish and she got back to me at home last night.'

'And?' Karen prompted.

'Apparently, they have had something like this happen before and there are several options.'

'Several? That sounds hopeful.'

'Not all of them apply in Mark's case—such as the option of waiting until his parents are better.'

'There are two reasons why that wouldn't work,' Karen agreed. 'First, that Christmas will be over by the time they're ready to travel.'

'And second that he won't be around for a second attempt next year,' Val finished sombrely. 'That's why she suggested that we sound him out about the idea of having one of his other wishes instead of visiting Father Christmas.'

Karen only had to see the expression on Val's face to know what the answer had been.

'There's no way he could be persuaded?' she said.

'No chance.' She shook her head. 'He said he'd already written to Father Christmas to tell him when he was coming. His parents posted the letter for him last week.'

'Oh, Lord.' Karen's throat closed up at the young lad's innocent faith and she railed inwardly at the misery caused by one careless driver.

'So. . .' She had to clear the huskiness from her voice before she could continue. 'What other options did they suggest?'

'She did say that the trip could take place as arranged if he went with other members of his family, but. . .' She shrugged.

'But we know that the only relatives he's got are his grandparents and *they* aren't capable of coping with him for more than a few hours, let alone a trip to a foreign country,' Karen continued despondently. 'So where does that leave him?'

'Obviously, for the sake of his morale, and Matthew's, he needs to go,' Valerie stated firmly. 'All we have to do now is find someone willing to give up their own Christmas plans and who is capable of accompanying a child with terminal brain cancer to visit Father Christmas in Lapland.'

Valerie's words were never far from Karen's thoughts that day.

Every time she happened to glance towards the corner of the ward where Mark and Matthew were, it seemed as if a little shadow chilled her heart.

She could remember Val telling her when she'd originally contacted Make-A-Wish to nominate Mark and, later, the news that he would be going on the trip of a lifetime with his parents.

It wasn't the first time that she'd seen the effect such a plan had on one of her little charges. Ever since the confirmation had come through, it was as if Mark had been supercharged with extra stamina—almost as if he was holding back the inevitable progress of the cancer which was killing him.

Now, with the cloud of uncertainty hanging over him, he was much quieter, and Karen had the feeling that he wasn't even allowing himself to hope too much.

It was Matthew's unexpected affinity which saved him. With no more than a hint from Karen, he managed to get Mark talking about the whole process of being chosen for a wish, and as he pestered him for more details about what the trip entailed gradually Mark's animation increased, until his deep depression was a thing of the past.

'We've *got* to get him on that plane,' Karen muttered to her friend when she reported back on Matthew's efforts, and demanded to know how far everyone had gone with alternative arrangements. 'Matthew has really put his heart and soul into keeping Mark's spirits up. I think he would be just as upset as Mark if he had to stay in hospital for Christmas instead of going away.'

'I'm expecting another phone call within the next half-hour,' Valerie informed her. 'If you take Mark across to visit his parents, that will put his mind at rest about their progress. Perhaps I'll have some better news for him when he comes back.'

Karen took the wheelchair across to Mark's bed, mentally crossing her fingers that Val was right.

'Right, young man. Your carriage awaits,' she announced. 'This is the mid-morning express, waiting to take you to see your mum and dad.'

Mark rolled over to face her, his little face still very solemn.

'They can't see me because they're in hospital too,' he murmured softly. 'They got smashed by the car.'

'Ah! But that doesn't stop you from going to visit them, does it?' Karen demanded playfully. 'I think it's only fair, don't you? After all, they came to visit you when you were too poorly to get out of bed, so it's *your* turn now.'

'Really?' he whispered, with dawning joy in his eyes. 'Can I really go and visit them?'

'Just as soon as we get you settled in here,' Karen confirmed as she patted the arm of the wheelchair. 'Are you ready?'

She helped him wrap his dressing-gown neatly and

retie the belt and then slid her arms around him, closing
her eyes briefly when she felt how frighteningly light
and fragile he was. Karen bit her lip and firmly banished
the image of the sturdy little body he should have had
as a seven-year-old, and swung him easily round into
the chair.

'Comfy?' she queried as she slid his feet into his
slippers and settled them on the rests.

'Mmm-hmm,' he murmured with a nod as he settled
his peaked cap more firmly over his stubbly regrowth,
and Karen swung the chair around. 'See you later,
Matthew,' he called, with a brief wave over his
shoulder.

'How far away is it?' he demanded in a stage whisper
when they were waiting with a small group of other
people for the lift to arrive. 'Will it take a long time to
get there? Do Mum and Dad know I'm coming?' The
final question held a note of uncertainty and he twisted
round to look up at her as she positioned the chair just
inside the lift doors.

'They know that you're coming some time today,'
she confirmed, stooping down to give their conversation
an air of privacy. 'But I didn't phone their wards to let
them know we were on our way—I thought you might
like to give them a surprise.'

'Yes! A surprise!' He gave her a beaming smile and
settled back to watch the changing numbers over the
door of the lift.

'Just two more corners,' Karen told him when she
eventually wheeled him towards the ward. 'We'll visit
your mum first and then go across the corridor to your
dad. OK?'

He was silent for a moment.

'Can you stop a minute?' Karen heard the urgency

in his voice and immediately guided the wheelchair into the side of the corridor and went to crouch in front of it.

'Is something the matter, Mark?' she questioned gently when she saw the worry on his face. 'Can I do anything to help?'

'Will they. . .?' He hesitated, then the words came out in a rush. 'Are Mum and Dad still all covered in blood?'

'Good gracious, no!' she exclaimed, careful not to laugh in case she damaged his childish feelings. 'They were all patched up and cleaned up as soon as they arrived at the hospital.'

'So. . .they'll still look like my mum and dad?'

'Of course they will,' she agreed. 'They've still got a lot of bumps and bruises and they both had to have stitches and plaster casts, but they're on the mend now.'

Karen kept her voice calm and soothing, knowing that Mark had already been told all these details but had obviously been too shocked to take them in at the time.

'They're not. . .they're not going to die?' His little voice was shaking as he voiced his deepest fear.

'No, Mark,' Karen said firmly, taking both his hands in hers and fixing his gaze with her own to reinforce her sincerity. 'They're not going to die.'

'You promise?' He looked at her with serious grey eyes, his little hands gripping hers tightly. 'You promise they're not going to die?'

'I promise,' she said, wishing it were possible to wrap him in a comforting hug and protect him from the chaos invading his young life. 'Now.' She straightened up and smiled down at his pale face before she finally disentangled their hands. 'Are you ready to give them a surprise?'

'Yeah!' he said gleefully, and he smiled up at her over his shoulder.

'You do realise that you've created another problem,' a husky voice greeted Karen as she went to make her farewells to Valerie later that afternoon before she went off duty.

'Oh!' Her hand leapt to her throat as she whirled to face the figure sitting quietly in the only comfortable chair in the room. 'You made me jump. I didn't see you there. . .' she babbled as her eyes made a lightning-fast survey of the long legs stretched out halfway across the cramped floor space and up over the lean expanse of torso to the broad shoulders slumped against the soft upholstery.

'I. . .I was looking for Valerie. . .Sister Clark,' she stammered, inwardly cursing herself for sounding such a ninny.

'Last seen heading off into the distance with murder in her eyes,' he murmured cryptically.

'Pardon?' Karen blinked, not certain that she'd heard him correctly.

'I believe it was a matter of a junior nurse being unfairly put upon by a less than diligent colleague,' he clarified dispassionately.

'That *would* put her on the warpath,' Karen agreed. 'She's always said that nursing's a hard enough job without the people you *should* be able to rely on making it any harder.'

'And I'll bet she includes consultants in that category, too,' he murmured, with a slight lift to the corners of his mouth.

'She certainly does,' Karen agreed as her eyes fixed

on the first glimpse of a smile he'd sent her way. 'Rank gets you no privileges with Sister Clark.'

'Thanks for the warning,' he said wryly. 'And here was I thinking that after years of work I would finally be assured of fawning consideration from the lowly masses.'

'Ha! You obviously haven't heard the one nurses tell about consultants being like monkeys—the higher up the tree they climb, the more you see of their less attractive aspects!'

There were several seconds of stunned silence before a husky chuckle turned into full-throated laughter.

'You nurses certainly know how to put us in our place,' he said drily when he'd caught his breath. 'No chance of over-inflated egos with wit like that around.'

'We do our best,' Karen replied. 'It helps us get our own back on some of the more pompous among the upper echelons.'

She suddenly realised that the man with whom she was happily trading conversation was a member of those upper echelons and hastily glanced down at the watch pinned to the front of her uniform to give her an excuse to look away from his keenly intelligent sapphire eyes.

'Well, it looks as if I'm going to have to wait until tomorrow to speak to Sister Clark,' she volunteered with a brief smile as she turned towards the door. 'I hope she doesn't keep you waiting long before she returns.'

'Actually, I was waiting for you,' he said quietly, and stopped her in her tracks.

'Me?' She pivoted round to face him again. 'Oh, yes. I remember now.' Her heart sank as she mentally replayed the words with which he'd greeted her arrival in the office. 'You said I'd created a problem?'

'You certainly have,' he confirmed seriously. 'I suggest you take a seat because I don't quite know how we're going to solve this one.'

'Oh, Lord,' she moaned half under her breath as she took the weight off her tired feet. 'Sitting down's fatal at the end of a shift. Now I won't want to stand up again.'

His stifled chuckle told her he'd heard every word in spite of the rustle of packages as she deposited her shopping bags by her feet.

'I have it on good authority that it was your idea to get Matthew to ask Mark lots of questions about his special wish,' he began formally.

'Yes,' she admitted honestly. 'Mark was so depressed that I thought it would get him thinking more positively if he told Matthew all about his trip.'

'It obviously worked beautifully,' he agreed with a sigh. 'The only problem now is that Matthew is desperate to go with him.'

'Oh, Mr Beckett, I'm so sorry.'

'It's not your fault. You weren't to know what a good salesman Mark would be, nor how starry-eyed my son would become when he heard all about it.' He pulled a wry face. 'God knows, he's had little enough joy and happiness in the last year,' he muttered.

'Do you want me to have a word with him?' she offered, her heart sinking anew at the thought of being the one to destroy his excitement. 'Perhaps I can let him down gently by telling him there's a long list of children waiting. . .'

'I'd rather you listened while I. . .' He paused and shook his head with an expression of disgust. 'No. It wouldn't be possible.'

'What?' Karen prompted, leaning forward eagerly.

'If you've got an idea that might help to divert his attention in some way. . .'

'As a matter of fact, I was wondering if you knew whether it would be possible for the two of them to go on the trip together.'

'Oh!' Karen slumped back in the chair with surprise. 'I never thought of that,' she said thoughtfully. 'That would certainly stop Matthew being disappointed—' She cut her own words off with a grunt of annoyance. 'I'd forgotten that the trips are all provided by the charity. They can only fund a trip when they've collected enough money and they aren't in a position to just add extra people—'

'What if I were to make a donation to the charity to cover the cost of the trip for both of the boys?' he broke in. 'In effect, that would mean that the money they'd already collected towards fulfilling Mark's wish would be available for another child. . .'

Karen considered his idea for several seconds, trying to find any flaws.

'As far as I can see, it seems to be the ideal solution,' she said at last, excitement colouring her voice. 'Obviously, you'd have to get in touch with the regional team and they'd have to put it to the organisers at the charity's head office in London. . .'

'What are you two plotting?' Valerie's voice startled both of them as she entered the room and made her way directly towards the kettle. 'By the expression on your faces, I think I'm going to need a strong cup of coffee to hear this one.'

'Actually,' Karen said excitedly, 'we might have solved a problem—or rather Mr Beckett might have.' She gestured for him to speak.

'As this isn't officially hospital business, do you think

it would be in order for the two of you to call me Nathan?' he said quietly, smiling up at Valerie as she handed him a steaming mug and shaking his head when she offered the sugar bowl.

'Oops,' said Karen when she saw the mug he was holding. 'I think you've given him the wrong one, Val.' She pointed at the motto emblazoned around the white china.

' ''Look busy. Here comes the Boss,'' ' his husky voice read out, and he joined in Val's laughter.

'Right.' Valerie shifted a top-heavy pile of papers and settled herself on the corner of the desk. 'What's been going on in here while I've been away?'

Karen knew Valerie meant the words as an innocent joke but suddenly she felt her face flaming, just as if. . . as if she and Mr Beckett. . .Nathan. . .had been. . .

'We think we might have found a way to sort out Mark's problem.' His deep tones broke into her frantic thoughts. 'Have you any idea whether Make-A-Wish would have any objection if I was to make a donation to cover the cost of Mark's trip and include enough so that Matthew could go with him?'

'I've no idea.' Valerie sounded quite taken aback for a minute, then a smile spread swiftly over her face before she leant across to rummage about for a small address book in one of the desk drawers. 'I've got the home number of one of the regional team in here. Do you want me to give her a ring straight away?'

'Can you give us a minute to think about all the ramifications?' he cautioned. 'At the moment, I take it you're no further forward in organising Mark's existing trip?'

'No,' she confirmed. 'We've been stuck over the problem of someone to travel with him. It's been a nightmare. We'd have any number of people only too willing to go on a holiday to Lapland for Christmas, but once you point out that they'd have to be taking care of a seriously ill little boy twenty-four hours a day and providing him with enthusiastic companionship the numbers tend to drop rapidly.'

'I expect another factor is that most people want to be with their own families at Christmas,' he commented quietly. 'That would narrow the field down even more.'

'It had actually narrowed the number down to nil, until you came up with this idea,' Valerie began gleefully, only to lose her smile a second later. 'Except. . . how on earth would you cope with the two of them single-handed? Matthew will have finished his latest course of chemo but he'll still be pretty steam-rollered by the side-effects, and although Mark is very little trouble as long as he's having a good spell. . .'

'*I* could go,' Karen heard a voice offer, and it wasn't until the two of them turned to look at her that she was horrified to realise that *she* had spoken the words.

'Karen! Of course. . .!' Valerie was beaming.

'That's very generous of you, but what about your own plans for Christmas?' Nathan's husky voice broke in over Val's delight. 'Shouldn't you ask your family whether they mind you disappearing over the holiday period?'

'Oh, that's no problem,' her superior said airily before Karen had a chance to draw breath. 'Karen hasn't got any family so she usually volunteers to work over family-type holidays to give other staff time off.'

Karen winced inwardly at Valerie's bald-sounding words and caught a brief glimpse of curiosity in a pair of deep blue eyes before it was swiftly hidden. She was only grateful that the topic of her family—or rather her lack of it—was dropped in favour of the problem of the moment. Unfortunately, however, she had a feeling that the information Valerie had disclosed had just been filed away for future clarification. . .

'Right!' Val said enthusiastically as she pulled the telephone towards her and consulted the list of telephone numbers. 'Let's see if we can all go off duty tonight with this matter settled once and for all.'

'What have I let myself in for?' Karen groaned into the darkness as she lay sleepless in bed that night, knowing that she would be repeating the words over and over again before the trip finally took place.

It wasn't the idea of travelling to Lapland that was the problem, nor the fact that she would be helping to take care of two seriously ill children while travelling through a region where the temperatures regularly fell to minus fifteen degrees Celsius.

No, she sighed as she went over it in her mind for the umpteenth time; she could cope with all that while standing on her head if necessary. It was the thought that she would be accompanying a man who suddenly seemed to be the embodiment of her every adolescent dream that worried her; she was terrified that she would make an utter fool of herself.

'You don't even know if you *will* be going yet,' she reminded herself the next day as she waited to meet the regional representative of Make-A-Wish. 'For all you know, they'll take one look at you and throw up their hands in horror. . .'

But she knew they wouldn't. She'd met both of the hard-working women several times before when they'd been organising wishes for other children under her care, and she'd got on well with them.

'Perhaps Mr Beckett. . . Nathan. . .will find someone else to go with him so I don't have to go. . .' she muttered to herself, but she knew deep inside that she would be very disappointed if he did, especially as Make-A-Wish head office had approved of their plans in principle.

'It isn't as if he even notices me—he certainly doesn't waste any smiles until Val comes into the room. . .' She pressed her lips tightly together as she heard how sour she sounded and resolved that if that was the effect he was having on her it was time to put consultant oncologist Mr Nathan Beckett right out of her mind.

It was easier said than done.

No sooner had she decided to return to her former calm non-involvement with her colleagues, and Nathan Beckett in particular, than it seemed as if every time she turned around he was there in the ward.

It wasn't enough that he kept popping in at odd moments to spend as much time as possible with his son, now that Matthew was suffering from a miserable range of side-effects to the new cocktail of drugs being used for his chemotherapy; and it wasn't fair that whenever he was there at Matthew's bedside her eyes were drawn to the obvious closeness between the two of them as Nathan spent his time alternately entertaining Matthew to take his mind off his misery and sitting quietly just to keep him company.

Apart from that, he seemed to have a never-ending stream of patients to visit on the ward—either new admissions who needed his attention before their treatment started or those who were recovering from a surgical procedure or undergoing more long-term therapy.

'Right, Holly.' Karen beckoned the young student nurse over, not certain in her heart of hearts whether she was using Steven Collison's arrival as a teaching opportunity or as a possible buffer between herself and Nathan Beckett. 'I mentioned yesterday that Steven would be coming in and that he has had a Wilms' tumour diagnosed. Have you been able to find time to do any research on the condition?'

'Psst!'

The noise behind them drew them both around to face the young man who had just arrived.

'Hey, Nurse,' he volunteered with a grin. 'If she's going to grill you about it, just ask me and I'll tell you anything you need to know.'

Holly grew quite pink and flustered.

'Thank you, Mr. . .?' she began.

'Collison. Ted Collison.' He beamed at the two of them. 'It's my son, Steven, you're talking about.' He gestured towards the little boy lying placidly across his mother's lap, his blond head propped in the curve of her arm.

'And you've been doing some research of your own,' Karen guessed.

'Right!' He nodded. 'I've always believed that ignorance is more frightening than knowledge, so as soon as Louise and I were told what was the matter with Steven we found out everything we could—like the fact that Wilms' tumour is a malignant renal tumour and seventy-five per cent of cases occur before the child is eight years of age.'

'Go to the top of the class,' Nathan said as he joined

the group. 'I can see I'm going to have to be on my toes with you.'

'Oh, no, Mr Beckett.' Louise Collison spoke for the first time, her voice pitched low so as not to disturb her son too much. 'You won't get any grief from us.'

'Certainly not,' the young father said as he offered his hand to be shaken. 'Louise and I are just so glad that the tumour was identified while it was classed as Group 1. If you hadn't been so good at your job, Steven wouldn't have been looking at a chance of a complete cure.'

'Well. . .' Nathan's voice sounded huskier than ever and Karen was amazed to see his cheeks darken with embarrassed colour as he turned away '. . .we've still got a long way to go before we can start talking about cures. In spite of the early diagnosis, Steven's still got a long road to travel.'

'We understand that,' the young man said in all seriousness. 'We realise that it'll take a combination of surgery, radiotherapy and chemotherapy to get him well again, but the books all agreed that the overall survival rate for Wilms' tumour is the highest among all childhood cancers—'

'In the meantime,' Karen broke in, moved to save Nathan's blushes, 'Nurse Burton will be taking special care of Steven while he's on the ward, which is why she's been making a special study of Wilms' tumours. This way, she'll be able to talk to you about what's happening to Steven, and make sure the other members of staff know about any special precautions.'

'Such as putting a sign on Steven's bed to warn people against putting any pressure on his abdomen,' Holly said as she smiled down at the silent four-year-old, who suddenly beamed back at her. 'You're a little sweetheart, aren't you?' she said as she bent her knees to bring herself down to his level, and then had to lean back quickly when his hand came out to try to catch the watch pinned to the front of her uniform.

'I can see I'm going to have to be on my toes with you, young man,' she said as she tapped his nose with the tip of one finger, and was rewarded with another cheeky smile.

'What's the drill for today, then?' Ted Collison wanted to know. 'Will you be starting on the blood tests?'

'Soon,' Nathan agreed. 'And we'll be sending him down for echograms to find out the exact extent of the tumour, and ultrasound to distinguish between a variety of renal masses so we know as much as possible what to expect before we operate.'

'Dad?' a little voice called just as the conversation reached a brief lull. When Nathan's head turned instantly towards the sound, Karen realised that among all the sounds in the ward he had recognised his son's voice calling him.

Karen watched as the young lad beckoned his father over, his little face quite grey under the influence of his chemotherapy cocktail.

'I'm sorry. Would you excuse me for a moment?' She watched as Nathan dragged his worried gaze back to the Collison family to make his apologies.

'You go ahead, Doctor,' Louise Collison urged. 'You've told us enough so that we know what to expect, and we can always ask one of the nurses to contact you if we're worried, can't we?'

'Of course you can,' Nathan agreed with a distracted smile. 'Apart from that, I'm in and out of the ward at intervals most days so I'm rarely far away.'

Mr Collison waited until Nathan was out of earshot before he spoke again.

'Nurse? Did that little lad call Mr Beckett Dad?' he demanded softly, and his expression changed to one of horror when he read the confirmation in Karen's face without her having to say a word. 'My God!' he breathed. 'How on earth does he cope with having his own child going through this? I couldn't take the pressure of knowing that if anything went wrong it would be all my fault. . .'

'On the other hand,' Karen suggested quietly, 'just think how wonderful it would be to know that you were able to take care of your own child and give him the best of attention.'

'Still—' he shook his head '—I don't envy him.'

CHAPTER THREE

'ALL right, my sweetheart?' Karen crooned as she stroked Steven Collison's feverish forehead with a cool, damp cloth. 'I hope you're feeling easier now. Look, here comes Mummy with your cuddly rabbit.'

She had the satisfaction of seeing the little lad's expression lighten as he caught sight of the bedraggled toy that the approaching young woman was carrying.

'Have you finished?' Louise Collison whispered. 'I'm sorry to be such a wimp but I can't bear it when you have to do that part.'

'We have to do the gastric suction after operations like Steven's otherwise he'd end up in trouble from distension or vomiting,' Karen explained gently.

'Oh, don't get me wrong. I know it has to be done,' the young woman said hastily. 'I've been through so many awful things with him during the course of chemotherapy before the surgery, but *that's* one of the things that really makes me cringe.'

'I've noticed,' Karen admitted wryly, and glanced towards the precious rabbit now tucked securely in her son's grasp.

'*That's* why you sent me on the wild-goose chase to find Mr Loppy,' she murmured. 'Thanks!'

'It won't be for much longer,' Karen reassured her as she noted the volume in the appropriate column on his chart and entered the equivalent intravenous fluids Nathan had designated to replace it. 'The anti-cancer drugs had done a marvellous job of shrinking the tumour

and he came through the operation brilliantly. Mr
Beckett is so delighted with Steven's progress that he'll
soon be starting him on oral feeding again—then you
won't need excuses any more.'

She gathered up the covered tray and moved aside
with an understanding smile so that Steven's mother
could move closer.

'He *is* doing well, isn't he?' Louise Collison's voice
made Karen pause on her way to the sluice. It held an
understandable trace of worry although she was obviously trying to hide it from her son. 'I know Mr Beckett
has explained everything to Ted and me, and he's been
very good about spending so much time with us, but. . .'

'You're worried that you're making a nuisance of
yourself when he's got so many other patients under
his care?' Karen suggested.

'Exactly!' Louise Collison blinked in surprise.

'I'm not a mind-reader,' Karen laughed. 'It's the
same thing that everyone feels. As far as *they're* concerned, their child is the most important patient in the
world, and they can't believe that the consultant sees it
the same way.'

'But he does, doesn't he?' the young woman said
thoughtfully. 'He really *cares* about each one of his
patients.'

'He does,' Karen agreed. 'But then, our Mr Beckett
is a very special man.'

She saw the sudden smile which crossed Louise
Collison's face just before the prickling of the tiny hairs
on the back of her neck alerted her to a presence
behind her.

'With a testimonial like that—' Nathan Beckett's
husky voice was laughter-filled '—how can I
go wrong?'

Karen whirled round to face him, her face red as she juggled to balance the tray she still carried.

'I'm sorry, sir. I didn't know you were there.' She dared a lightning glance towards his face and surprised a fugitive gleam of laughter in his deep blue eyes before they once again matched his calm expression.

'And they say eavesdroppers never hear well of themselves,' he commented to an openly grinning Mrs Collison.

'It must be good to find out what the nurses really think of you,' she retorted.

'Only when they say something nice,' Karen retaliated, her nerves sensitive to the thought that he might be laughing at her embarrassment. 'He could hardly have known what I was going to say before I said it.'

'Ah, but with our Staff Nurse March it was a foregone conclusion,' he replied easily, catching her disconcerted gaze with the power of his stunning sapphire eyes. 'Everyone on the ward could tell you that if she doesn't have anything good to say about you she doesn't say anything at all!'

Her cheeks felt as if they were about to burst into flames but Karen was held as though hypnotised.

The sounds of the busy ward faded into insignificance as she became conscious only of the man standing in front of her, his height and breadth radiating power as he held her undivided attention.

'Well. . .' Louise Collison's voice reached her from a long way away '. . .at least it shows she's a good judge of character, because Ted and I totally agree with her.'

Karen blinked and saw Nathan Beckett jerk slightly, as if he'd only just realised what was happening between them.

'All I can say is thank you both for the compliment,'

he murmured with a slight bow, his voice huskier than usual and a faint trace of colour highlighting the lean planes of his cheeks.

'Excuse me,' Karen croaked as she fixed her gaze on the forgotten tray grasped tightly between her hands. 'I must take this. . .' She fled without finishing the sentence, her brain totally unable to formulate a coherent thought.

'Dammit!' she muttered as her trembling hands dealt with matters in the sluice, grateful that she was totally alone. Only one other person had ever had such an effect on her—her ex-fiancé, Gareth Jenkins—but even with him she'd never been shaken like this; never been made so totally aware of another human being that the rest of the world faded into insignificance.

Even so, just the thought of Gareth was enough to calm her racing pulse and bring her feet firmly down to the ground. The heartbreak he had caused her had made her vow that she would never let herself be vulnerable to a handsome face and a facile turn of phrase again.

'Pull yourself together,' she hissed under her breath as she disposed of her gloves. 'You've got no call to go all starry-eyed over his sweet-talk. It wasn't personal—he was only being pleasant to Steven's mother. . .' And she straightened her shoulders and pushed out through the doors and back onto the ward.

'Staff Nurse?'

In spite of her self-exhortation just half an hour ago, Karen couldn't help the sudden twist of awareness deep inside her when she heard his husky voice calling her, and it took all her determination to turn and face him with a calm expression.

'Yes, sir?' She was conscious of the fact that her chin had lifted and her shoulders were squared as though to make the most of her slight five feet three inches in the face of his more imposing frame. 'Can I help you?'

There was a slight pause and she saw one eyebrow lift in response to her coolness. When he spoke, his dispassionate voice matched her own. 'Sister Clark is waiting to speak to us in her office.' And he gestured for her to lead the way across the corridor.

'Oh!' Karen couldn't help her natural enthusiasm breaking through her tenuous control. 'Has she heard from the regional organisers? Has a decision been made?'

'Why don't we go through and find out?' he suggested, his calmness unruffled.

'Val...er...Sister Clark.' She stumbled over her words in her eagerness to find out what the news was. 'You wanted to see me...us? Is it about Mark's trip?'

'Here.' Valerie Clark turned to hold a mug out. 'Grab this and sit down before you explode with curiosity!'

Karen gingerly took possession of the handle turned towards her and glanced automatically at the motto with a distracted grin. ' "I'm not old, I'm a recycled teen-ager," ' she read out, and couldn't help chuckling. 'Where do you find these?' She sank gratefully into the chair and slid her feet out of her shoes.

'Tom seems to bring home an inexhaustible supply,' Val explained as she waved Nathan Beckett into the comfortable chair before she handed him a bright yellow mug. 'Some of them are a bit pointed.' She turned her own round to show the two of them the legend, 'I'm not fat, I'm just short for my weight,' then gasped and shot a horrified glance at the mug in Nathan's long-fingered hand.

'I see what you mean.' His husky voice held more than a hint of laughter when he glanced down at the motto on his own mug and a wash of colour heightened his cheekbones.

Karen was intrigued and couldn't wait for him to read it out, but was disappointed when Val broke in hurriedly to tell them the latest news.

'After meeting the two of you, the regional team went to speak to Mark's parents about your suggestion and then spoke to Mark too. Then it was Matthew's turn to tell them what he thought about it.'

'I suppose that meeting was to make certain that it really *was* what he wanted to do?' Nathan queried.

'Yes.' Valerie smiled wryly. 'Apparently, some families find out that they will be included in any trip and try to persuade the child to say, for example, that he really wants to go to the Bahamas for a fortnight, instead of wanting to meet his local football hero.

'Anyway,' she continued, 'the upshot is that head office were delighted to give the go-ahead for Mark's trip and, just a few minutes ago, they received confirmation from the tour company that the extra flight and accommodation is available and has been booked so that Matthew can go too.'

'Oh, that's fantastic,' Karen said, her voice raised with enthusiasm. 'Have the boys been told? And Mark's parents?'

'Not yet. I only got the phone call a few minutes ago. If you like, the two of you can break the news and take Mark up to tell his parents.'

'I assume that Make-A-Wish will let us know all the arrangements?'

Nathan's tone was so matter-of-fact that Karen suddenly felt like shaking him to see if she could force a reaction out of him. The most she'd ever witnessed was one brief laugh and the smiles he bestowed on his young charges.

Was he totally unaffected by the excitement of it all? How much did it take to get him worked up?

Suddenly she had a mental image of Nathan Beckett as he would look when he really got worked up, his colour heightened by something more than a funny slogan on a coffee-mug, his thick blond hair in disarray and his dark sapphire eyes half closed with arousal as he concentrated intently on the object of his desire. . .

'Karen?'

The husky voice hardly intruded on her daydream; in fact it almost seemed to be an integral part of it as she imagined the words he would say as he leant over her and began to arouse her too. . .

'Karen!'

Valerie's voice broke sharply into the scene and Karen found herself blinking in confusion as she tried to face two identical frowns.

'I'm sorry. . .I was. . .' What? What on earth could she say? I was busily imagining what our consultant oncologist would look like when he makes love? 'What did you say?' she asked swiftly before her thoughts got her into any more trouble.

'Mr Beckett asked. . .'

'Nathan. . .remember?' he reminded Valerie with a smile.

'Nathan,' she repeated with a smile, 'asked if you've got a current passport.'

'Oh. Yes. I got a ten-year one several years ago.'

The memory of her excitement when she'd filled in the application form and had her photograph taken for it was an uncomfortable one, interspersed as it was with mental images of Gareth and his suggestion that now they were engaged they could go away for a holiday together. . .

'Do we need any visas to go to Finland?' she asked, determined to shut the lid on that particular Pandora's box with the sheer weight of practicalities.

'Not coming from England,' Val confirmed.

'What about currency and so on?'

'It will all be taken care of by Make-A-Wish, right down to the travel to and from the airport.'

'So all I have to do now is try to persuade the ward sister to arrange the duty roster to give me time off to go,' Karen said cheekily.

'That's a point,' Nathan broke in. 'Because I've started work here earlier than I was expecting, I'm not absolutely certain where I stand over holiday entitlement. I'd better find out in case I have to practise grovelling to get what I want.'

'That reminds me.' Val clicked her fingers. 'Have you heard how Mr Firzal is getting on? The last we heard was when he was released to go home.'

'He's made a good recovery,' Nathan confirmed. 'I went to see him the other day and he actually looks younger now than when I met him at my interview.'

'Do you think he regrets deciding to retire completely?' Karen asked. 'He really seemed to enjoy the job and everyone loved him. I would have thought it would have been a terrible shock to his system to give it all up like that.'

'I know what you mean,' he replied thoughtfully. 'I think he does miss it, but he realises that retirement was the only answer. He could hardly have had the hospital hanging on waiting to see how long it was going to take him to get back to work.'

'Do you think. . .?' She hesitated, then plunged on. 'Would he be interested in providing cover for you in case the department needed help while you're away?'

'Listen to her!' Valerie laughed. 'Given half a chance, she'd take over the running of the hospital!'

Nathan's mouth curved into an answering smile.

'Actually, it's not a bad idea,' he admitted. 'He'd probably be delighted that we'd thought to ask him, and there's no reason why he should actually need to do very much—we don't routinely schedule our type of surgery for Christmas, so that it isn't so traumatic for the patients and their families.'

'So you think he would be willing to be on call for you?'

'It's certainly worth pursuing—after all, he knows more about the department than anyone else! I'll take a side-trip to Administration and put the idea to them in person before I mention it to him in case they have any legal problems with it.'

'Do you want to sort that out before we tell the boys about the trip?' Karen suggested.

'Good Lord, no. There's no urgency for that. Let's go and give them the good news.' He pushed himself upright and turned to deposit his cup on the tray in the corner. 'Unless there's anything further you wanted to say?' he asked Val.

'No. I've given you the good news, so the rest of it is between you and Make-A-Wish.'

'Right.' His long legs took him across the room, a touch of impatience in his stride. 'Let's go and see Mark and Matthew.'

Karen slid her feet back into her shoes and retrieved the empty mug from the floor beside her chair.

'Leave that. I'll put it away. . .' Val began, but it was

too late. Karen was already across the small room and reaching for the bright yellow mug to read the words which had seemed to cause the two of them so much embarrassment.

'Val!' Karen exclaimed, her tone a mixture of shock and amusement when she turned the mug round to reveal the stark black words. 'How could you have given this one to him?' She began to chuckle as she held it up in front of her friend. ' ''Most sex maniacs drink out of yellow mugs,'' ' she read aloud.

'Don't!' Val groaned. 'I didn't remember what was written on it until he looked at it and by then it was too late!'

Karen was still stifling her chuckles when she followed Nathan Beckett across to his son's bed.

By the time she joined him, he was sitting on the side closest to Mark's bed and the two youngsters were watching her when she perched herself like the other half of a mirror image on the edge of Mark's bed.

'Right, boys. Staff Nurse March and I have just had some news and we thought that you might like to hear it.'

'Is it about my mum and dad?' Mark butted in anxiously. 'Are they all right?'

'They're fine, Mark,' Karen reassured him as she wrapped one arm around his slender shoulders in a swift hug. 'The news isn't about them, but we thought you could go up to tell them as soon as we've told you.'

'What is it, then? What's the news?'

'Do you remember writing a letter for your mum and dad to post to a foreign country?' Nathan prompted.

For a moment, Mark looked at him blankly, then they saw remembrance dawn.

'Yes! I wrote to Father Christmas to tell him I was coming to see him.'

'Well, do you think you could help Matthew to write a letter like yours? Because you're going to have your wish just as Make-A-Wish promised, and Matthew is going with you too.'

'Oh, wow!' Mark breathed, his eyes growing larger and larger. 'Oh, wow, Matthew. Did you hear that? We're going to see Father Christmas and snow and reindeer and sleighs and. . .and everything!'

For several minutes there was pandemonium as the enormity of the coming adventure registered with the two of them and they reacted with typically childish whoops of delight.

Suddenly the whole ward was involved as word of what was going on spread from bed to bed until they were enveloped in a wonderful carnival atmosphere. All the children who were fit enough to walk came over to speak to the two boys, and the rest sent their visitors to find out all the details and bring them back.

'When are you going?' one young patient with a head hidden under a bulky bandage demanded. 'Today?'

'No. Not today. We're going. . .when *are* we going, Dad?' Matthew demanded, his voice so full of animation that he hardly seemed like the same child who had been suffering so badly with the side-effects of chemotherapy.

'Not until just before Christmas,' Nathan said with a smile. 'That's so that we'll be there for Christmas Day.'

'Are you coming too?' he said, obviously not taking in all the details in his excitement.

'Of course I am. I want to see Father Christmas too!'

Both boys giggled at his injured tone and it was some time before the ward finally settled down into some sort of normality again and it was time for Mark to be taken to break the news to his parents.

Over the last couple of days, with the visits from the regional representatives from the charity, Karen seemed to have spent quite some time taking the plucky lad backwards and forwards in his wheelchair and they were developing a good relationship which augured well for their journey together.

The staff on the two adult surgical wards had managed to rearrange things so that it was easier for the Hoopers to receive visitors and to see each other.

Karen's visit that day with Mark was an emotional one and she was glad that she was able to leave the three of them together for a while to talk privately.

'Nurse?' Mark called when they'd been speaking for some time. 'Can you come here a minute?'

Karen had been telling the staff on each ward what was going on and, at Mark's urgent-sounding summons, made a swift farewell to her opposite number.

'You look worried, half-pint. What's the problem?'

'Will I be able to telephone my mum and dad when we're away to tell them what's happening?'

'Oh, I expect so,' Karen reassured him. 'And you'll be able to have lots of photos taken so you can bring them back to show everybody.'

His worried frown disappeared but it was soon obvious that the excitement had made him very tired.

'Hey, half-pint. Time to give your mum and dad a hug. I expect Matthew's waiting to hear what they said.'

With the Hoopers' thanks for her part in making the trip possible still in her ears, and a promise to visit again soon, it was time for Karen and Mark to make their way back to their own ward.

'Phew!' Nathan breathed as he sat back down on the

edge of his son's bed while Karen settled Mark under his own covers. 'I feel as if I've been picked up by a tornado, whirled around until I'm dizzy and then dropped back down again!'

'Welcome to life on Paediatrics, Toto!' she smiled wryly. 'We seem to lurch from high to low and back again with frightening speed around here.'

'Dad?' a sleepy voice murmured. 'I've been thinking. . .'

'What about?' Nathan leant forward to stroke his son's head gently, his eyes fixed intently on the innocent little face outlined in the soft glow of the light above his bed, and Karen found herself fighting to swallow around the lump in her throat.

'How can I be going to see Father Christmas when I'm in hospital having chemo-ferapy?'

Karen watched a smile tug at the corner of his mouth but when he spoke he was taking his son's question seriously.

'Don't you worry about that, Matthew,' he said reassuringly. 'You'll have finished the treatment before you go. All you've got to think about is writing your letter to Father Christmas to tell him you're coming to visit.'

The two boys were asleep almost before he'd finished speaking but Karen found herself lingering, as though needing a few moments of peace in the turmoil of the daily routine of the ward.

Nathan reached forward to turn the light off over his son's head, the click sounding loud in the evening quiet.

As she watched, he straightened up, drew in a deep breath and released it as a sigh as he dropped his head back tiredly.

'Any chance of a cup of coffee?' he murmured, then

flicked a swift glance towards her when Karen couldn't help the brief chuckle which escaped her control.

'Any particular mug?' she questioned softly.

There was a brief silence and then she heard an answering chuckle.

'You saw it,' he said, the words husky in the shadows. 'I thought I'd managed to dispose of it so Sister Clark wouldn't be embarrassed.'

'*That's* why I made certain to look at it,' Karen murmured quietly as they made their way towards the pool of light coming through the observation window which made up one wall of Sister's office. 'Now I have the ammunition to tease her for ever!'

'It doesn't seem fair,' Louise Collison muttered as she tried to soothe Steven after another bout of sickness. 'He came through the surgery so well and now he has to go through chemo again.'

'We've got to make certain there weren't any cancer cells left to multiply,' Karen said patiently as she cleared away the mess. 'That's part of the reason why the survival rate for Wilms' tumour is so good—because we use a belt-and-braces technique to knock it out completely.'

'It just seems so hard on him,' the young woman wailed softly as she looked down at his exhausted little face. 'He's still so little to go through all this. . .and his hair was just beginning to grow back, too.'

'You'll be having to pay out for haircuts soon enough,' Karen said reassuringly. '*And* you'll be at your wits' end trying to get him to sit still long enough!'

'True.' She managed to raise a half-smile. 'At the moment he's so quiet and still that it terrifies me—it's so unlike him. I suppose I'll look back on this time with disbelief when he's tearing round like a maniac again!'

'Chin up,' Karen encouraged. 'You're over halfway there and it looks as if you're going to be one of the lucky families.' She couldn't help her eyes straying across to the other side of the ward where Mark and Matthew's beds stood side by side.

Mark had been so much better since his trip to see Father Christmas had been confirmed, almost as if he was once again drawing strength from the excitement of the plans. Unfortunately, Karen knew that it was likely to be a short-lived reprieve, as his latest scan had shown that his tumour had started increasing in size again.

'It doesn't seem fair,' Karen echoed Louise Collison's words as she heard the latest news about Mark's condition. 'We thought the first operation on his tumour had removed enough of it for the chemo to do the mopping up but then he had to go through surgery all over again when it came back.'

'That's the trouble with gliomas in that region of the brain,' Val agreed. 'They wrap themselves around it like tentacles and the poor surgeon has to choose between trying to get every last bit out so there isn't any left to start growing again, and going too far and causing terrible damage to the control mechanisms of the brain.'

'I know,' Karen said tiredly. 'I just hate watching the children deteriorate, knowing that all we can do is offer pain relief until the inevitable happens.'

'Still. Look on the bright side. If you open any nursing manual written more than ten years ago, it will state unequivocally that surgical removal of brain-stem gliomas is not possible. It's only the technological advances of this decade which have made such a difference.'

'The CT scans and MRI and ultrasound aspirators haven't done Mark much good. He's been through it twice and he's still dying,' Karen detailed grimly.

'But if we hadn't tried he would already be dead,' Nathan's husky voice pointed out as he joined the two of them in the office. 'The operations have given him an extra eighteen months so far, and each operation will have taught the surgeons just a bit more so that they will be able to help their next patient, and then the next.'

'But so much of that eighteen months has been spent having chemo and surgery and radiotherapy.' Karen's frustration showed in her tone. 'What sort of gain is that?'

'Enough so that in a couple of weeks he'll still be alive to go to meet Father Christmas,' he reminded her quietly. 'Sometimes, the miracles don't happen. You just have to measure the benefits in small steps.'

'Oh, I'm sorry.' Karen dropped her head into her hands and speared her fingers through the thickness of her hair. 'Sometimes, when everything we do seems so futile, it gets to me. I feel like screaming in frustration when I see an otherwise perfect seven-year-old dying and I know there's nothing I can do to stop it. I don't think I'll ever be able to accept the idea of children dying.'

'And yet you specialised in paediatric nursing?' There was a question in his voice.

'And she's damn good at it too,' Val interjected warmly, making Karen's cheeks burn. 'I have lots of nurses coming through my ward during their training but very few of them have what it takes.'

'Is it something you can tell just by looking at them, or does it come with time?' Nathan quizzed.

'Usually, it's something special inside them. . .an empathy.'

'Is that how you see it?' He turned his serious face towards Karen. 'Is that what made you choose paediatrics?'

'I felt that children with diseases such as cancer had drawn the short stick. They were at the beginning of their lives and I felt. . .' Karen paused and squeezed her eyes closed while she concentrated on her thoughts and feelings. 'I just knew that I had to do everything I could to help them,' she said finally, her dark brown eyes opening suddenly to fix on Nathan's intent sapphire gaze. 'If all I can do for them is talk to them and make them comfortable, then I'll do it, because that's what they need.'

A strange silence fell over the small room as though it were waiting for something important to happen, and then Nathan smiled at her, his eyes warming her as the pleasure in them poured out towards her like sunshine.

'Karen March—' his husky voice finally broke the silence '—I'm glad you're on my team.'

CHAPTER FOUR

THE next couple of days were relatively quiet for Karen.

She used her day off to take advantage of a closing-down sale in a sporting-goods shop and stock up on several heavy jumpers and some thermal underwear, ready for the sub-zero temperatures she could expect once they got to Finland.

'Not what you'd call sexy, are they?' Valerie sniffed when Karen showed her. 'In fact, I'd class them as real passion killers!'

'As long as they stop me from freezing my bits off, I don't care what they look like,' she retorted. 'Something which will cover me from my nose to my toes will be just the job.'

'But what about all your pretty underwear?' her friend persisted. 'If you're going away with Mr Sex-on-a-stick. . .'

'Who won't be the least bit interested in seeing how many shades of blue I go when I get too cold,' Karen finished impatiently. 'Honestly, Val. The two of us are going to take two very sick little boys to see Father Christmas because it will probably be the last chance they have, and trying to catch sight of each other in our underwear will be the furthest thing from our minds.'

'More fool you!' Valerie muttered in disgust. 'All you have to do is see what he does for a suit to know that he'd be even better in the flesh—and you're turning down the chance to find out!'

'Val!' Karen exclaimed. Her tone was shocked but

she didn't dare say anything else for a second in case her friend realised that the shock was caused by the sharp twist of arousal which had spiralled deep inside her at the thought of seeing Nathan Beckett's naked body.

'I know you don't go lusting after the doctors the way some of the nurses do, but couldn't you make an exception in his case?' she wheedled with a wicked glint in her eye. 'You aren't likely to get a better chance. . .'

Karen didn't dignify the suggestion with a reply because she wasn't able to think of one which wouldn't give away the fact that for the first time since Gareth's cruelty she actually *was* interested in a man, *was* interested in seeing what he looked like when his powerful body wasn't camouflaged by an expensive suit and tie.

Later that day, she was afraid that Val was going to bring the topic up again in front of Nathan himself, but all she did was mention the shopping Karen had done.

'Have you thought about the clothes the two boys will need to go away?' Val prompted. 'I doubt if either of them will have anything suitable—children rarely manage to fit into anything a second year running.'

'Lord! I hadn't thought of that,' Nathan said with a grimace. 'And I'm hopeless at choosing anything for Matthew unless he's there to try it on.'

'What about Mark? Had his parents started getting things ready for his trip before the accident?' Karen asked. 'Would it be a good idea if I went up and had a word with them?'

'You do that,' Nathan agreed with relief. 'And if he still needs some new things perhaps I could give you a list for Matthew and you could get them at the same time?'

Karen almost objected to his blatant attempt at

passing the buck but she had the strange feeling that his out-of-his-depth expression wasn't feigned. Because he was a man who seemed so eminently in charge whatever he did, the fact that there were some things which left him feeling helpless, some things for which he would welcome her assistance, gave him an extra dimension.

'Have you any idea what Matthew's measurements are?' she said briskly to cover the treacherous melting sensation starting around her heart.

'Measurements of what?' An endearing flush deepened over his cheekbones and he was avoiding meeting her eyes.

'Don't worry about it,' she said with mock resignation. 'If someone can find me a tape-measure, I'll do both of them at the same time.'

As it turned out, both boys needed new clothes for the trip, Mark's parents having planned to make the new wardrobe part of his surprise.

'They'll need extra-warm underwear and thick winter jumpers because neither of them is fit enough to race around to keep warm,' Karen reported back to Nathan. 'Apparently, the tour organisers will be providing each of us with special padded all-in-one suits and boots.'

Nathan perused the list she'd drawn up then looked at her with a plea in his eyes.

'Where did you say this shop is? Do they have this sort of thing in there, in these sizes?'

'Oh, give me that!' she groaned as she reached out for the piece of paper. 'All right—I'll do the shopping.'

'No. I can manage,' he said defensively as he held it easily out of her reach. 'Just tell me where the shop is. I can follow a list as well as the next person.'

'If you're certain.' Her tone was dubious. 'Just have

a quick read and see if there's anything you don't understand—other than my writing!'

'It all seems fairly straightforward, especially as the
two of them seem to be the same size for a lot of things,'
he said confidently. 'Except. . . If they're both going to
be having the same clothes from the same shop, how
are we ever going to tell them apart?'

'Buy them in different colours?' Karen suggested.

'What colours?'

'Whatever the shop sells.'

'But how do I choose which colour for which boy?'

He was beginning to sound hopelessly lost again and
Karen's soft heart took over.

'Men!' she exclaimed in an exasperated voice as she
whipped the list out of his hand. 'I'll meet you outside
the shop at nine o'clock tomorrow morning—if that fits
in with your timetable?'

'Oh!' He rubbed the palm of one hand over his face
tiredly while he thought. 'I can't remember,' he sighed
as he shrugged his broad shoulders. 'I'll have to get my
secretary to give you a ring if I can't make it. She keeps
my diary and she'll be able to suggest another time if
that doesn't fit.'

'Don't forget that the shop won't be restocking,'
Karen warned him. 'If they run out of the things you
want before we get there, you're going to have to pay
twice the price elsewhere.'

'Right,' he said blankly, and she was hard put to it
not to laugh. It was obvious that he'd never thought
about such things before. Exactly how long had he had
custody of Matthew, and who had been organising his
shopping trips before Karen appeared in their lives? she
wondered.

*   *   *

'Come on,' Karen muttered as she jiggled from one foot to the other in an attempt to stay warm, moving in time to the beat of the music from the speakers inside the shop.

This exposed corner of the rather run-down end of town seemed to be catching the sharp edge of the wind but she didn't dare go inside to get warm because she was afraid that if she did she'd never meet up with Nathan Beckett to get the shopping done.

As it was, she'd been standing here so long while shoppers swirled around her in a hurried stream to get out of the cold that she was beginning to get some very funny looks from some of the passing men. . .

An extra-vicious gust of wind nearly swept her knitted hat off her head and she had to pull it off completely before she could settle it comfortably over her hair again.

She glanced down at her watch again and groaned silently. Just five more minutes, that's all. Then I'm going inside the nearest café to thaw out. . .

'Karen?' The familiar husky voice stopped her in her tracks and she whirled round to face him.

'Where have you. . .?' She paused suddenly to peer up at him from under the fluffy edge of her knitted hat, her uncertainty swiftly turning to stunned amazement. 'Nathan?' she questioned faintly, and she could feel her eyes growing wider as she took in his changed appearance.

Where was the tall, austere figure in the smart suits who strode to and fro through her life at the hospital? This man was dressed in a cream-coloured guernsey sweater over an open-necked dark blue shirt that picked up the spectacular colour of his sapphire eyes, his long, muscular legs encased in well-worn denim jeans that revealed as much as they concealed.

For several seconds the two of them stood silently looking at each other as though they could hardly believe what they were seeing, before the situation suddenly struck them as funny and they chuckled simultaneously.

'You look so—'

'I didn't recognise—'

They laughed again, then he gestured for her to continue.

'I think we've *both* been standing around waiting for each other,' she said wryly.

'And while I was waiting for Staff Nurse March to arrive I watched a very irate young woman hopping about to pop music while some terrible man kept her waiting in the cold.'

'While I've been waiting for a consultant oncologist to arrive and worrying about being accosted by some hunk in faded denims. . .' She stopped speaking with a gulp but it was too late as the words seemed to echo for ever in the silence.

Suddenly the sound of his uninhibited laughter rang off the shop-fronts and Karen's warmly gloved hands tugged her hat down even further over her ears in an attempt at hiding her blushes.

'A hunk?' he spluttered. 'That's the first time in my life that anyone's ever called me *that*!'

'I'm sorry,' she mumbled, furious at her unruly tongue, but the difference in his appearance had been such a shock that she hadn't had time to gather her thoughts. 'I didn't mean to. . .'

'Oh, don't *spoil* it!' he teased. 'I was quite enjoying the novelty—especially at my age!'

'Oh, shut up, Methuselah,' she snapped crossly as she turned towards the shop door. 'Let's get this shopping done before the shop closes down completely.'

She pushed the door open and was instantly surrounded by noise.

Her elbow was grabbed from behind and she turned in time to see Nathan's open amazement.

'Good God!' He murmured his horror in her ear, the warmth of his breath reaching her through the fibres of her fluffy hat as he leant close enough not to have to shout.

'It's one way to attract the younger customers.' She returned the manoeuvre, conscious that he had to lean down a long way for her to reach his ear.

'Will this take long?' His eyebrows were drawn down into a pained expression as the next record began and a series of lights began to flash on and off in time to the beat.

'I hope not,' she mouthed over her shoulder as she beckoned him to follow her towards the racks of clothes for younger children.

They'd just made the last decision over the necessary clothing for the two boys when there was a shout from the other side of the shop and several customers began to stare at some sort of disturbance.

After an initial glance, Karen was inclined to dismiss it as youthful exuberance, until the look on the customers' faces registered.

'Nathan. . .?' she began, her hand reaching out to grasp his elbow, but he was already moving towards the circle of people forming between the racks of clothing and equipment.

'Excuse me!' The authority in his raised voice drew nearly every eye towards him for a second before they

returned to their fascination with the scene at their feet.
'Where is the manager?' he demanded forcefully as he
shouldered his way through the goggling bystanders.
'Get that noise turned off. Now!'

'Hey! Who do you think you are?' one youth
challenged as Nathan grasped his shoulder to move
him aside.

'I'm a doctor,' he replied fiercely. 'Now, let me
through!'

Suddenly a path opened up and Karen was able to
see just what she'd feared—a youngster on the floor
almost completely surrounded by spectators while he
suffered a seizure of some sort.

'Get a pencil,' someone shouted into the sudden
silence as the sound system was switched off. 'You've
got to get it between his teeth.'

'No!' Nathan's voice countermanded swiftly as he
reached the youngster and knelt down beside him.
'Don't touch him. Just move the racks aside to give
him room.'

Karen had followed him through the gap he'd carved
between the fascinated bystanders and arrived beside
him in time to watch him make a swift assessment of
the lad in spite of his violent movements.

'Do any of you know him?' she asked quietly, her
eyes travelling around the sheepish circle of faces to
catch a response from two youngsters of about the same
age. 'You do?' she queried, then raised her voice to the
rest of the group. 'If the rest of you would like to
continue with your shopping. . . Give the lad a bit of
privacy, please!'

There were a few mutters and the shuffling of feet
as the red-faced spectators dragged themselves away
from the free drama going on in their midst.

'Right, lads,' she began when the rest had moved away. 'Do you know if he's on any medicine for seizures? Have you seen this happen before?'

'No,' the taller one answered in a shaky voice. 'I've never seen Andy do this before.'

'How was he when you met up this morning? Did he seem OK—not complaining of a headache or anything?'

'No. He was fine right until we came in here and then he was on the floor.'

'Do you know if he's taken anything he shouldn't? Any drugs?' Nathan fired at them, the fact that he was kneeling on the floor not detracting from his air of command.

'No!' the smaller one answered angrily. 'We don't do drugs. They mess your head up.'

'OK.' Nathan nodded. 'Did either of you see what happened? Did you see him fall down?'

They looked at each other and shook their heads.

'Right. I need your help.' Nathan changed tack. 'Could one of you ask if someone's phoned for an ambulance and come back with the answer? If it's on its way, could the other one go to the shop door to let the ambulancemen know where your friend is?'

Karen waited until they'd both disappeared between the racks of clothing before she spoke.

'How is he?' She crouched down beside him, still clutching the forgotten basket of clothing.

'He's coming out of the clonic phase. I don't think he's done any physical damage, apart from biting his tongue—he must have gone down between the racks without hitting any of them, and the floor's carpeted. Apart from that, I can't find any unusual neck stiffness to suggest meningitis, he's not wearing any sort of medi-

cal identification to show he's epileptic and there are
no needle tracks.'

'Any idea what might have caused it to happen?' she
questioned as she helped Nathan to turn the youngster
onto his side, then scrabbled for a small packet of paper
hankies in her bag which she offered to Nathan to mop
the lad's face with.

'At the moment, in the absence of any other information, the only thing I can think of that might have
triggered it is the music and those wretched flashing
lights.' He flicked a glare towards the offending appar-
atus suspended from the ceiling of the shop. 'It's bad
enough having it at discos and such—at least susceptible people can avoid them. But when you can't even
go shopping without running the risk of having an attack
triggered. . .'

His angry mutter was cut short by the arrival of an
ambulanceman.

'Good morning, sir. Can you tell me what happened
to the lad?'

'Morning.' Nathan looked up from his position beside
the youngster and Karen saw him gently stroke the back
of his young patient's hand to soothe him when he
reacted to the sound of the new voice. 'This young man
is Andy. He came in here shopping with two friends
and had a seizure. He's come out of the clonic phase.
No obvious injuries apart from a bitten tongue.'

'Does he have a history of seizures?' the ambulanceman asked as he put down his bag and reached
for the stretcher his colleague had brought. 'I take it
from your knowledge of the situation that he's
your son?'

'No. He's not mine. Just another customer in
the shop.'

'But. . .' The poor man's puzzlement was obvious.

'I'm a paediatrician,' Nathan supplied, and gave a brief smile when he saw the man's face clear.

'Well, he chose the right company to be taken ill in,' the other ambulanceman commented. 'Not many patients get instant attention on the spot.'

Andy's two friends were hovering in the background while he was being loaded onto the stretcher and, seeing the worry on their faces, Karen made her way over to them.

'He's going to be all right, you know,' she said, trying to reassure them. 'They'll check him over at the hospital to make sure he's on the mend. Have you had a chance to get hold of either of his parents yet? They'll need to know what's happened so that they can meet him at the hospital.'

'Won't they let us take him home when they've looked at him?' the shorter lad demanded. 'Then his mum and dad wouldn't have to know about this.'

'Of course his parents will have to know what happened,' Karen retorted in surprise. 'The doctor at the hospital will have to tell them what to look out for in case it happens again.'

'Told you,' the taller one muttered in an aside. 'I told you that's what would happen.'

Karen's eyes travelled from one to the other as a suspicion began to form in her mind.

'You're not supposed to be here, are you?' she accused softly. 'Are you supposed to be in school?'

They glanced at each other guiltily so that she knew the answer before they nodded.

'Our teacher's off sick today and we were supposed to go with another class for extra sports until lunchtime.'

'So you thought the three of you could do a bit

of Christmas shopping and get back to school in time for lunch and afternoon lessons without anyone finding out?'

'Yeah. Only now we've got no chance. Andy's parents, our parents and the school are all going to freak on us just because we didn't want to freeze our b... Sorry!' he muttered.

'Well.' Karen glanced over at the stretcher and watched for a second as Nathan bent to say something to Andy. 'Do the two of you want to go with him to the hospital?'

'Can we?' A trace of boyish excitement surfaced through their teenage anguish.

'Oh, I expect it can be arranged,' she said as she led the way over to the two ambulancemen. 'Do you two need anything carried out to the vehicle?' She smiled as she indicated the pair following on her heels like a pair of eager puppies. 'I've got two willing porters here who'd like to do something to help their friend.'

Within minutes Andy had been carried out and the ambulance was on its way. The last view Karen had of his two friends was just as the doors were swung closed, their young faces positively glowing with excitement and hero worship as the ambulanceman taking care of Andy explained what he was doing for him.

'Now, let's get this shopping finished,' Nathan said as he led the way back into the shop. 'Have you got the basket of clothes?'

'I left it with the young woman behind the cash desk. She said she'd look after it until we came back,' Karen volunteered as she followed him.

They'd almost reached the counter when the music and lights suddenly began again, seeming louder than ever.

'I don't believe it,' Nathan growled, his face thunder-ous as he stalked the last few strides towards the smiling young woman. 'Please will you get the manager?' he said politely, his voice raised loud enough to be heard clearly over the renewed din.

One glance at his expression was enough to send her scurrying away to do his bidding.

'Can I help you?' a thin young man said as soon as he arrived, one hand reaching for the basket overflowing with clothing which Karen had rested on the edge of the counter to relieve her hand.

'I certainly hope so,' Nathan said clearly, placing one hand on the pile of purchases to prevent the young man from pulling it towards him. 'But first will you please turn that noise down so that I can speak to you without having to shout?'

'It's all right.' He smiled weakly. 'I can soon ring these up for you. . .' And he reached out again towards the basket.

'I don't think you heard me.' Nathan's tone was steely. 'I said, can you turn the noise down, please— unless you want the whole shop to hear when I have to shout at you to tell you what I think?'

Karen saw the young man blink and a slight tinge of colour creep up over his prominent Adam's apple and into cheeks still bearing the scars of teenage acne.

Without another word he shut his mouth tightly and turned towards the controls behind him.

'And while you're doing that you could turn off those infernal lights too,' Nathan added, just in time to have his words heard right around the suddenly quiet shop.

'Right, sir,' the young man began when he turned back to face them, tight-lipped with subdued anger. 'How may I help you?'

'Can I ask you a question?' Nathan said pleasantly. 'Were you in the shop at any time during the last half-hour?'

'Yes. I've been here since half past eight this morning.'

'In which case you will know that a young man has just had to be taken to hospital after suffering a seizure in the shop?'

'Yes. I phoned for the ambulance.'

'Thank you,' Nathan said courteously. 'You were very prompt. Unfortunately, there is a possibility that it was *your* fault that you had to call the ambulance.'

'What?' he gasped. 'But I wasn't anywhere near him!'

'Maybe not,' Nathan conceded. 'But you were responsible for the volume of the noise that thing puts out and for switching on those flashing lights, weren't you?'

'Well, yes...but...'

Out of the corner of her eye, Karen saw a rather overweight gentleman stop just out of the young man's sight, obviously listening to the conversation taking place at the counter.

'And didn't you realise that they can be the trigger which brings on seizures such as the one young Andy just suffered? That if the seizure had been severe enough he could even have died in here?'

Karen laid a calming hand on Nathan's sleeve.

'Apart from that,' she said softly, 'you sell top-quality goods in this shop and they are expensive to buy. This means that it is usually adults who come in here to pay for things, even if it's their children who've chosen them.'

'Well, yes,' he conceded, responding to her gentler method.

'Don't you think that your aggressively loud music might be having an effect on the number of people coming in here to buy—?'

'In fact,' the overweight gentleman broke in, 'it's probably one of the reasons why trade is so bad that I'm having to close this branch down.'

'Mr Adler!' the young man gasped, and turned pale. 'I didn't know you were there.'

'Obviously not, young man,' he replied bluntly before turning to Karen and Nathan. 'I was driving past the shop when I saw the ambulance outside. Would you mind telling me what's been happening in here this morning?'

'Coffee?' Nathan suggested as he shifted one of the bulky carrier bags to his other hand. 'I think we deserve a cup.'

'Lovely. Thank you,' she agreed after a quick glance at her watch. There was still plenty of time before she had to be at the hospital for the late shift.

As she followed in the wake of his broad shoulders, Karen's heart gave a little skip at the thought that their shopping trip wasn't over yet. She was thoroughly enjoying Nathan's company—in spite of the traumas.

'Can I get you anything to eat?' he offered as they queued by the long counter with their tray. 'It's nearly lunchtime and it would save you having to eat at the hospital. Besides, it would give us time to talk about the trip. . .'

Once he'd given her a cast-iron excuse to spend more time with him, she found herself falling in with his suggestion all too readily.

Soon they were settled at a small table in a shadowy corner at the back, their parcels piled on a spare chair as they tucked into a surprisingly tasty lasagne with a crisp side-salad.

'I was ready for this,' Nathan admitted after the first couple of mouthfuls.

'Shopping can be exhausting,' Karen agreed with a straight face. 'It's the effort of making all those decisions. . .'

'Cheek!' he exclaimed. 'I'll have you know that those parcels are heavy.'

'Especially as you insisted on carrying all of them.'

'It's my gentlemanly instincts.'

'Ah! Now I understand why you're so exhausted. Gentlemanly instincts will do that to you every time!'

Karen glanced up in time to watch laughter take over his face, the fan of fine lines beside his eyes accenting the deepening hue of his dark blue eyes.

'Karen, eat,' he ordered, pointing at her plate. 'Your tongue is too smart for your own good.'

'Well, we wouldn't have had so many parcels if you hadn't decided to take a stand in that shop.'

'If *I* couldn't do it, who would?' he questioned. 'It was just sheer chance that the shop owner came in while we were telling that young sprog what we thought of the noise and the lights.'

'Still. One day, when he thinks about it, he'll realise that your complaint was instrumental in giving him another chance to make the shop profitable. At least the owner is giving him another chance—without the dreadful lights and music!'

Karen looked at the pile of parcels and thought with pleasure of the extra items the owner had insisted on giving to them by way of a thank-you for their help.

'I think Mark and Matthew will be pleased with the clothes,' she said. 'It's amazing how the youngsters today are so fashion-conscious. At their age, all I was interested in was being busy, not what I was wearing while I was playing.'

'And that's so long ago,' he teased with a twinkle in his eye. 'You must be all of...what, twenty-two, twenty-three?'

'Twenty-seven,' Karen corrected him stiffly as she kept her eyes firmly fixed on her plate. 'I didn't start my nursing training straight from school.'

'Why not? Couldn't you decide what you wanted to do?' The question was apparently casual but Karen was beginning to know how Nathan's mind worked and he very rarely asked idle questions.

'I knew what I wanted to do but...family matters prevented me from doing it.'

As he turned her words over in his mind, the silence began to stretch uncomfortably between them, and Karen found herself saying more than she'd intended just to break it.

'I'd been at Charing Cross Hospital for a year and a half when my mother had a stroke. I had to stop my training to take care of her and my father.'

'I'm sorry,' he began gently. 'At least your nursing would have come in handy...'

'I was training as a doctor,' she said flatly, the old heartache of having to give up her dream lending a bitter edge to her voice.

'Was there no way you could have continued?'

'Not according to my father.' She raised her eyes to his, expecting to see...what? Pity that she'd lost her dream? Scorn that she hadn't found some way to achieve it?

What she found was calm understanding that some things were beyond one's control and she drew in a deep breath, flooded with gratitude that at last she'd found someone she could talk to—Gareth certainly hadn't wanted to listen to her woes.

'I take it he insisted you gave up your training?'

'Yes.' Her mouth twisted in a wry grimace. 'According to Father, as their daughter it was my duty to take care of them.'

'How badly affected was your mother?'

'Bedridden, incontinent and unable to speak coherently.'

'Damn, that's hard.'

'Especially when it goes on twenty-four hours a day.' Karen shook her head at the memories.

'What? You must have had some help?'

'That would have cost money. You don't have to pay a daughter the going rate—in fact you don't have to pay her anything except houskeeping money to buy the essentials.'

'Good God!' He was silent for a moment. 'What happened when she died? Is that when you did your nursing?'

'No. That's when my night shift ended. I still had to keep house for him—until his mistress managed to persuade him to allow her to move in. Then, as soon as he'd added her name to all the legal documents, like the deeds of the house and his bank accounts, she took the lot away from him.' She glanced up from her preoccupation with shredding a paper napkin. 'I think it was the shame of it that made him commit suicide.'

This time she didn't attempt to break the silence

between them. She'd already told him far more than she'd ever told anyone else.

'So all the time you were taking care of your mother and the house he was spending his time and his money on another woman?'

'If I'd known, I'd have walked out and let him employ a housekeeper, but I was counting on him keeping his promises. He'd been helping to finance me through medical school—paying for my living expenses, books, travel that weren't covered by grants and loans. He said that if I looked after Mother he'd continue doing that when I returned to my studies. When it came down to it. . .' She shrugged.

'Didn't you have anyone you could turn to? Other relatives? Friends?'

'I'd just got engaged before Mother had the stroke and he wasn't very understanding when Father insisted I came back home. He sent a letter asking for his ring back the day Mother died.'

'Bastard,' Nathan muttered in disgust, his eyes very dark.

'Oh, the timing wasn't deliberate,' Karen explained evenly. 'He'd found someone else he wanted to give it to—another student doctor who shared his aspirations.'

'Saying I'm sorry seems inadequate, somehow. Especially when I feel far more like finding the miserable worm and rearranging his features for him. What a pathetic specimen of humanity!'

Karen was surprised into a chuckle.

'Thank you.' She smiled. 'That's the first time I've been able to think about the whole sorry mess without wanting to smash something. Just the thought of someone wanting to do it for me. . .'

She chuckled again as her mood lightened still

further. 'Not that dumping me did him much good,' she added with a wicked grin. 'Within a couple of months, his new fiancée had dumped him for a better prospect and refused to give him the ring back!'

CHAPTER FIVE

By THE time they'd had a sinfully rich dessert and a second cup of coffee it was almost time to go to the hospital.

'Do you need to go home first?' Nathan asked politely. 'I could take you there in the car then get you to the hospital in plenty of time for your shift.'

'No, thanks.' Karen smiled. 'I've got a clean uniform in my locker. All I have to do is hope that no one makes a mess of it partway through the shift because it's my spare one.'

'What would be the best thing to do with all the shopping?' he asked as he retrieved one bag which had slithered off the pile and under the table. 'Have you got room for it all at the hospital or should I lock it away in the boot of my car?'

'I think we need to sort it out a bit,' Karen suggested as they made their way towards the car park. 'If we separate out the bags with the boys' things so we can take them in to show them, we can then take our own things home after work.'

'OK. I'll leave it up to you.' He unlocked the boot of the car and deposited all the bags. 'Have a quick rummage round in that lot and then it's time we were on our way.'

There was some sort of hold-up on the journey, so that they only reached the hospital car park with ten minutes to spare. Karen was trying to see her watch and juggling with two bulging bags while Nathan locked up.

'Give me those and get yourself off to change into your uniform. I'll bring these up to show them in about an hour, when you've had time to get organised.'

'Are you sure? It doesn't seem fair to leave you with—'

'Consultants are allowed a little more leeway,' he said as his long fingers coped easily with the loops of the bags. 'Get going.'

'OK. Thanks.' She relinquished the last one. 'See you later,' Karen called over her shoulder as she hurried towards the entrance. Her heart gave another of those silly little skips at the thought that she would be seeing him again in an hour and she couldn't help the smile which lifted the corners of her mouth.

'And what were *you* doing getting out of Mr Beckett's car with bags of shopping?' Holly Burton challenged as Karen set foot on the ward with just minutes to spare. 'How long have the two of you had something going? I haven't heard anything on the grapevine yet.'

'What's this?' Valerie demanded. 'Have I missed out on the latest gossip?'

'Karen's got something going with Mr Sex-on-a-stick,' Holly announced with a delighted grin. 'I was just arriving for work when I saw her getting out of his car and passing over the shopping bags for him to carry.'

'The only *thing* I've got going with Mr Beckett is the fact that we had to go to buy some thermal clothing for Mark and Matthew for their trip,' Karen said defensively, knowing all too well how quickly rumours could spread if they weren't corrected straight away. 'He'll be bringing the shopping up to show them in a little while.'

'Oh, yes!' Holly's tone was sceptical. 'And I suppose buying clothes for two little boys is the reason why you had a smile on your face like the cat that got the cream.'

'Rubbish,' Karen said hotly. 'I was running across the car park so I'd have time to change into my uniform.'

'That's the first time I've seen someone so happy to come to work that they smiled that way,' Holly taunted.

'Holly, there's no point in trying to get blood out of a stone. If Karen wants to keep something close to her chest, you might as well give it up as a bad job. Just bide your time,' Val said with a knowing smile. 'Time will tell.'

Karen groaned. 'When Sister Clark starts on the clichés, it's time to go, Nurse Burton.'

'Right, Staff Nurse March. I'm right behind you.' And they set off around the ward to check up on their charges before the food trolleys arrived.

In the end it was nearly halfway through Karen's shift before Nathan finally arrived on the ward. He'd managed to send a message to his son to let him know that he wouldn't be able to visit him before he went to sleep, but it was only through the infamous hospital grapevine that she'd heard that the reason why he hadn't come any earlier was that he'd been delayed in Theatre.

'Psst!'

Karen looked up from the pile of paperwork she was finishing but couldn't immediately see one of the patients trying to attract her attention. The ward was lit just by night lights and everyone seemed to be fast asleep.

'Psst!'

This time Karen was able to get a rough idea of which direction the the sound was coming from and got up to go over to check on the beds in the area nearest to the ward doors.

'Is everyone asleep?' a husky voice demanded from the shadows.

'Those of us who aren't having heart attacks,' Karen whispered back as Nathan emerged into the half-light from behind a curtain. 'What on earth are you doing?'

'I've brought the bags of clothing up for Mark and Matthew but I didn't want them to catch sight of them tonight and perhaps get too excited to sleep.'

'Good idea. As it was, we had to disappoint Matthew when we told him you couldn't make it.'

'Damn.' He raked his fingers through his hair and left it in deep furrows across the top of his head. 'I thought the move here would let me have more time with him, but it certainly didn't work out that way today.'

'He was very good about it. Told us you would have to pay a forfeit for missing bedtime.'

She saw the gentle smile soften his features.

'It's a game we play,' he explained. 'He'll be thinking up a suitable forfeit to make up for my absence.'

'What sort of thing?' Karen was intrigued.

'Oh, the chance to beat me at the latest computer game or smuggling in a slice of pizza. . .that sort of thing.'

'That doesn't sound like much of a punishment.' She chuckled quietly in deference to the sleeping figures surrounding them. 'That sounds as if you enjoy the punishment just as much as he does.'

'Who said women had a monopoly on clever ideas?' he challenged. 'Now, where am I going to put the boys' clothes? Is there somewhere on the ward where they could be locked away until tomorrow?'

'Where are they at the moment?'

'Just inside the ward doors, in the corner.'

'If you'll hold the fort here for a minute, I'll go and put them away in my locker. They'll be safe there until I come on duty tomorrow.'

'Right. While you're doing that, I'll go through to Sister's office and see if I can scrounge a cup of coffee.'

When she slipped back into the ward a few minutes later she could see where Nathan was, the light above his son's bed turned down low so that it didn't disturb him while his father sat silently beside him, his eyes fixed on the still figure under the rumpled bedclothes.

Karen turned away to give him the semblance of privacy and had to swallow a lump the size of a golf ball as she made her way into the office.

The kettle had only just switched itself off so she spooned instant coffee into two mugs and topped them off with a dollop of milk.

As she carefully lifted the two full mugs over to the desk, she smiled when she realised that she'd narrowly avoided giving him the bright yellow one again, this time managing to choose two with silly animal cartoons.

'I hope one of those is for me,' he murmured as he joined her in the office. 'I only meant to take a quick peep at him while the kettle boiled.'

'No problem,' Karen dismissed. 'It was just switching itself off when I got back.'

'Did everything fit?' He sank down into the chair that she was coming to think of as his and took a sip.

'It was a tight squeeze. The lockers aren't very big and some of that thermal stuff is very bulky.'

'So we'll all look like the Michelin man.' He shrugged.

'As long as we *all* look like him,' Karen countered. 'Some people I know are tall enough to wear that stuff and still look good while the rest of us are lumbering about with all the grace of a walrus.'

He gave a husky chuckle and they both grew silent, sipping occasionally from their gently steaming mugs.

'I needed this,' he murmured when he finally drained the last of the coffee. 'Not just the drink but the company. You're a very restful person.'

His eyes met hers over the top of the mug she had just been going to empty and her hand tightened on the handle as a swift shaft of pleasure pierced her.

'That's a relief,' she murmured when she finally found her voice. 'It's not long before we're going to be thrown together for several days with two over-excited young boys. It would terrible if we drove each other round the bend.'

Once again her nerves were treated to the velvet stroke of his husky chuckle. 'I suppose you're right but I'm sure we'd have made the best of it for the boys' sake.'

For the boys' sake.

The phrase began to haunt Karen more and more the closer the departure date for the trip came. It didn't matter what she was doing, at the hospital or during her free time—she could hear the tolerant laughter in his voice when he'd said it.

It coloured her pleasure in Mark and Matthew's excitement when they were shown their new wardrobe, and the thanks Mr and Mrs Hooper heaped on her for helping to make their son's last Christmas such a happy one. It even began to interfere with her sleep, the words echoing hollowly through her dreams.

It was only when she was looking in the box in the back of her wardrobe for the large washbag she used to take on holiday that everything finally fell into place.

'Where's the wretched thing hiding?' she muttered as she scrabbled through the odds and ends she'd never got around to unpacking—partly because she didn't have anywhere to put them in her tiny flatlet.

'Good Lord. . .what on earth did I ever keep that for?' She brandished a single glove before aiming it at the small bin she kept just behind the bedroom door. 'What else am I going to find if I keep digging in here. . .? Oh. . .' She sat back on her heels with a thump, the latest item held gingerly between her fingertips.

Gareth's photo.

She'd thought she'd got rid of them all in an orgy of destruction ages ago but her subconscious must have deliberately forgotten this last memento.

His dark eyes gazed out at her. She'd always thought that the hint of laughter in them made it seem as if he was sharing a delicious secret with her, a special bond just between the two of them. Once, she'd only had to look at the photo to be reminded of how much she'd lost, the tears welling as she relived how much it had hurt. . . But now it was gone!

For the first time, she could look at his once beloved face and see the trace of self-conscious smugness in his expression. Oh, he'd been good-looking all right—and he'd known it. But looking at him didn't hurt any more. Thinking of him just evoked a nostalgic smile and a distinct feeling of gratitude that in the end she'd escaped with nothing more permanent than a badly bruised ego.

Why hadn't she realised it before? It was so long since he'd broken their engagement, told her he'd found someone else. Had she nurtured her disappointment so carefully that she hadn't even realised that the bruises had healed long ago—or had something else brought about the healing? *Someone* else. . .?

She stood up slowly and took the couple of steps which brought her to the rubbish bin behind the door. Her fingers opened and she watched the photo settle on top of a couple of used tissues and balls of cotton wool without a single pang.

For the first time in a week she woke after a good night's sleep and was filled with a feeling of expectancy—as if something wonderful was about to happen.

She had always enjoyed her job but for some reason today was special and she couldn't wait to get to the hospital.

'You look happy—won some money on the lottery, have you?' one of the young porters demanded with a wink. 'If you need some ideas for spending it, just let me know.'

'I'm sure you're full of ideas but I'm sorry I haven't got the money to finance them,' Karen quipped as she clipped the ward door open for him, ready for the trolley to come through.

'I suppose that means I'll have to keep looking for a wealthy woman to keep me in the luxury I'd like to become accustomed to,' he grumbled jokingly as he parked the trolley out of the way at the side of the ward and went to check his paperwork with Sister.

'Who's going for a ride?' Karen enquired.

'New one. Petra Agnelli. She's going down for an ultrasound scan.' Valerie glanced up from the details. 'She's three years old and they think she's got a tumour in her uterus.'

'Oh, God,' Karen breathed, suddenly feeling sick. 'I knew it was possible, theoretically, but I've never come across it at that age before. The family must be devastated.'

'It hasn't been confirmed yet, so as far as they know it's one of a list of possibilities.'

'Who's going down with her? Her mum?'

'And grandmother,' Val confirmed. 'Will you go and see if Holly's ready to accompany them down to Radiology? She did Italian at school and she remembers enough to speak to the family to tell them what's going on, so she'll be staying with them until they come back up to the ward.'

The results of Petra's preliminary tests were back later that day and were sufficiently worrying that Nathan was immediately involved in a meeting with the family to explain the next step.

'What's the news?' Karen demanded as soon as the meeting was over and Valerie returned to her office. She'd been hovering in the background hoping to see Nathan but he'd already left the department.

'Good and bad,' Val said as she settled herself behind the desk. 'She's definitely got some sort of growth there but it doesn't look as if it's spread to the surrounding structures.'

'So, what's been decided? Surgical biopsy?'

'Yes. Mr Beckett's gone off to see how fast he can fit her into his list.' She glanced up as Holly joined them. 'Well done, Holly. Mr Beckett was impressed by the way you kept your cool when Petra's grandmother went off the deep end.'

'Poor lady,' Holly said sympathetically. 'Apparently, it's the first time she's been able to afford to come over from Italy to get to know her granddaughter and she ends up hearing that she might have cancer.' Holly's own eyes looked a little pink, but Karen could see that she was coping well.

'Your time in this ward is being a bit of a baptism

of fire,' she commented as Val reached out to answer the phone. 'Has it managed to change your mind about specialising in paediatrics?'

'No,' Holly returned firmly. 'If anything, it's made me more determined.' Her chin came up and the lingering tearfulness was banished by her air of resolution. 'What will happen next, when Mr Beckett takes her down to Theatre?'

'He'll do the surgical biopsy under a general anaesthetic and the sample will be sent straight up to the labs while he waits for the results. Depending on what they find, he'll decide what sort of treatment she needs and carry on straight away.'

'So Petra will still be unconscious on the operating table while the labs examine the tissue?'

'Yes. It saves her having to have a second anaesthetic if they do have to do a surgical removal.'

'So she could end up having a total hysterectomy at three years of age?' she asked quietly.

'It's possible, depending on what they find.'

'Is there no other way of dealing with it?' Holly was beginning to sound choked up again. 'It's such an irrevocable step.'

'If it's the only way of saving her life. . .' Karen pointed out gently, knowing that she didn't need to finish the sentence.

'But she hasn't had the biopsy yet so I'll be keeping my fingers crossed,' Holly said stubbornly.

'As long as you can cope if that method doesn't work,' Karen murmured under her breath as Holly went to continue her duties on the ward.

'Karen?' Valerie's voice broke in on her thoughts. 'That was Mr Beckett. They need all the pre-op preparations done on Petra Agnelli. They're going to add her on to the end of today's list.'

'Another good and bad scenario,' Karen said wryly.

'I know what you mean. It's good that the family won't have to wait too long to find out what's the matter with her but bad that it's happening so fast because it means that he thinks it's that serious. Right.' She planted both hands flat on top of the paperwork on her desk and levered herself to her feet. 'Action stations.'

Karen was just getting ready to go home when she heard the sound of someone trying to stifle tears behind the locked door of one of the toilet cubicles.

'Are you all right in there?' she said softly, with a sneaking suspicion that she knew who was in there and what her problem was. 'Anything I can do to help?'

'No, thanks,' a tearful whisper floated over the door. 'I'll be OK.'

As she waited, there was the sound of vigorous nose-blowing then the flush was pulled before the lock went back.

'I thought it was you.' Karen smiled sympathetically as Holly appeared. 'Did you get it out of your system?'

'I think so.' The young woman bent to splash her reddened eyes with cold water and patted her face dry with a paper towel. 'How do you cope?' she demanded shakily. 'Did you cry at first or am I a wimp?'

'I still cry sometimes—especially when it's one of my special favourites. But these days I can usually manage to bottle it up until I get home.'

They both fell silent as they each donned warm clothing ready for the journey home, but Karen took her time, knowing instinctively that Holly needed a friendly ear for a little while longer.

'Poor little scrap,' she sniffed. 'She's brought her favourite doll into hospital with her and she was cuddling it when she was waiting to be anaesthetised. She'll never be able to have a baby of her own now.'

'Oh, Holly. You'll have to learn to let it go.' Karen put an arm around the younger woman's shoulders. 'The family will be offered counselling and they'll be able to tell her right from the start that she'll be able to adopt a family if she wants one.'

'But it's not the same, is it?' Holly challenged. 'It won't be *her* child.'

'That depends on your point of view. I must admit, I've always thought that a mother was the person who brought up a child rather than the one who just brought them into the world. If you can do both successfully, you're one of the lucky ones.'

'But. . .'

'I know it's a tragedy in its own way,' Karen continued, ignoring Holly's emotional attempt at interrupting. 'But when she's older I think Petra will realise how lucky she was that her GP was quick enough off the mark to get her here in time to save her life. At least this way she'll be alive to make her own choices.'

'I'm sorry. You're right.' Holly blew her nose again. 'I'm just being totally unprofessional about the whole thing.'

'It's not unprofessional, it's a good sign. It shows that you care,' Karen reassured her, with a final squeeze of her shoulders. 'Now, if you want some advice, get home as quickly as you can, have a hot bath, a warm meal and a large mug of hot chocolate before you go to bed. The world won't be any different when you wake up, but after a good night's sleep at least you'll have the energy to deal with it.'

'Thanks, Karen. I needed to get it off my chest.'

'I know. We've all been there.' Karen's smile was wry. 'Now, go home!'

She turned to face the mirror over the basin and realised just how tired she looked. This morning she'd woken up so full of enthusiasm, so sure that today something special was going to happen, so certain that it had something to do with Nathan.

Her hands gripped the cold white porcelain edge of the basin as she remembered his face when he'd arrived to tell Petra's mother and grandmother what was wrong with their precious little girl. He'd been hurting almost as much as if she were his own daughter.

Her heart clenched tightly as she relived the urge she'd felt at that moment to go to him and hold him, to share his pain the way she would if she loved him. . .

The realisation was slow in dawning on her and when it did she stepped back sharply, horrified by the direction her thoughts had taken. She wasn't falling in love with Nathan Beckett. She couldn't be—not if they were going to be going away together in just a few days. How could she possibly cope with four days in his company?

Her mind darted about frantically in an attempt to find a way out, knowing all the time that there was no way she could back out now. Mark and Matthew were depending on her to go with them.

She stood still and breathed deeply as she got herself back under control, and finally she was able to make the final admission—she didn't want to back out of the trip because she was longing for the chance to spend those four days in Nathan's company; to travel with him and talk to him and help him to take care of his son. . .

Her new calmness firmly in place, Karen emerged into the corridor.

'I was just about to send someone in there,' a husky voice said right behind her and she spun to face him, feeling as guilty as if he had been able to eavesdrop on her recent thoughts about him.

'Nathan!' A smile spread across her face when she saw him leaning nonchalantly against the wall and pleasure filled her at his unexpected presence. 'Why were you going to send someone in?'

'Well, I can't hang around out here for very long without it having a serious effect on my reputation!'

'Idiot! That wasn't what I meant, and you know it!' she exclaimed, her tiredness disappearing in an instant as her pulse rate increased. 'Why were you waiting?'

'I've been trying to catch up with you all day, but it's been chaos.' He drew in a deep breath and shouldered himself away from the wall.

Karen felt her smile fade.

'Petra,' she murmured, and knew they were on the same wavelength when he grimaced. 'She's still in Intensive Care so I haven't had a chance to see her notes. How is she?'

'Does the phrase as well as can be expected ring any bells?' He gestured for her to accompany him on his way out of the department.

'How bad was it?' she prompted.

'Bad enough.' His tone was grim as he continued almost angrily. 'Sometimes I hate playing God with the patients' lives. I hate the uncertainty, not knowing whether I've left too many of the cells behind so that the cancer will come back, or if I've taken too much tissue away and permanently damaged the patient's quality of life.'

He grabbed her elbow and swung her to face him. 'There are no dotted lines when you're in there, with labels saying ''so far and no further'',' he said, his voice almost accusatory.

Karen stood still under the furious glare of his dark blue eyes, knowing that he couldn't be aware of how tightly his hand was gripping her arm.

'I can't remember where I heard it,' she said softly, 'but someone once told me that even though medicine is a science nobody ever said it was an *exact* science.'

There was a moment's silence before he gave a brief chuckle and released her to rub both hands over his face. 'I'm sorry.' He sighed. 'I know I did what I had to for the sake of Petra's life, but just for a moment I found myself wondering whether I should take a chance and try to remove only the cervix in the hope that her uterus could be saved; but. . .' He shook his head.

'There are no guarantees that it wouldn't have been endangering her life further at a later date,' Karen finished. 'Nor that the radiotherapy and chemo wouldn't have made her sterile anyway, so you'd have been taking unnecessary risks with her health for the sake of a mythical future pregnancy.'

Her words ended in a strange silence and Karen suddenly wondered if she'd gone too far, been too outspoken.

'Thank you,' he said quietly, and sighed. 'Sometimes I need someone to put things into perspective and bring me back to earth.' He gave a tired grin. 'Come on. It's time we got out of this place. Anyone would think we couldn't bear to leave it!'

'Was there a particular reason why you wanted to speak to me?' Karen asked as they made their way out into the damp darkness.

'Hmm?' Nathan's hair gleamed under the lights as he turned questioningly towards her.

'You said you'd been trying to catch up with me,' she reminded him. 'Was it something to do with work?'

'Oh!' Remembrance struck him and he reached one hand into the inside pocket of his suit jacket. 'No. It was to tell you that these have arrived. . .' And he pulled out a folder containing the airline tickets and itinerary for their trip to Lapland.

'Oh, Mark.' His mother gave him a last hug, hiding her tearfulness behind a smile. 'Have a wonderful, magical trip. I'm just so sorry that your dad and I can't go with you.'

'Me too,' he mumbled. 'But Matthew said that Christmas won't wait for you to get better.'

'Matthew's quite right,' Mr Hooper agreed. 'And with the two of you together I'm not certain that Father Christmas knows what he's let himself in for!'

'Dad!'

'Oh, I think we'll manage to keep the two of them under control between the two of us,' Nathan said with an easy smile towards Karen. 'Perhaps we'll have to threaten them with having to eat with the reindeer!'

'Can we?' Matthew gazed up at him with shining eyes. 'Can we really eat with the reindeer, Dad?'

The four adults groaned.

'That was supposed to be a threat, not the promise of a treat,' Nathan grumbled while he tried unsuccessfully to hide a grin.

'Well, if everyone's finished making their goodbyes,' the voice of one of the members of the regional Wish team broke in, 'I think the taxi is loaded up with all the luggage and waiting to go.'

'Don't forget to send us a postcard from Father Christmas's post office,' Mark's father reminded him when he gave him a final one-armed hug.

'And take lots of photos to show us when you come home,' his mother murmured as she fussed with his brand-new brightly coloured bobble-hat. 'We love you, Mark.'

'Love you too,' he muttered as he threw his well-padded arms around her neck for a final squeeze.

'Your carriage awaits,' Karen announced as she brought the wheelchair across.

'And no wheelchair races down the corridors,' the ward sister warned Nathan and Karen with a sternly wagging finger.

As the two giggling boys were escorted out to the corridor she called a final reminder. 'Don't forget to look up at the window before you get into the taxi to see a surprise.'

Her final comment intrigued the boys enough to take their minds off the sadness of leaving Mark's parents behind.

'Do you know what she was talking about?' Karen murmured under the cover of boyish speculation.

'No idea.' Nathan shrugged. 'Whatever it is, it helped to get us out of there without drowning in tears.'

Karen and Nathan wheeled the two boys far enough across the parking area to be able to look up towards the windows of the Hoopers' wards and saw that a home-made poster had been stretched across the front of the building.

'Oh, wow!' Matthew breathed. 'Look at that!'

' "Give our love to Father Christmas," ' Mark read out.

This time it was Karen who felt the tears welling up

as she saw the sea of faces at every window and the forest of hands waving the two boys on their way. It seemed as if half of the hospital had turned out to wish the two of them a good trip.

'Did you know about this?' Nathan muttered, his cheeks slightly pink as he avoided meeting her eyes.

'No...but I think it's wonderful!' She gave him a distinctly wobbly smile, amused as she watched him try to hide his embarrassment.

'One last wave and then we've got to go,' Nathan declared briskly in a voice that emerged huskier than ever. 'We don't want to miss the plane.'

CHAPTER SIX

'IT's snowing!' the two boys chorused excitedly as the plane came in to land at Rovaniemi airport. 'It's really snowing!'

The two of them had been very good on the journey in spite of their excitement. Although the flight had lasted over two and a half hours, they'd happily watched the film being shown and had enjoyed their first introduction to airline food, but the highlight had undoubtedly been their visit to the cockpit of the plane to be introduced to the pilot.

As they taxied to a halt, their limited view of the Arctic twilight outside the small window showed them the bright lights of the terminal against millions of whirling white flakes, the effect magnified by the clouds of snow flung into the air by the power of the jet engines.

'It looks just like the little snow thing I got last Christmas!' Mark exclaimed. 'When I shake it, the snow flies around and around before it all lands on the little house again.'

There was a last reminder from the cabin staff to make sure that they hadn't left anything under the seats or in the storage lockers above before it was time to go.

Because of the boys' special needs, they were the first to leave the aircraft.

'Right. Who's first?' Nathan stood smiling in the gangway, the lights along the ceiling of the aircraft

striking gleams along the thick strands of blond hair
and making his dark eyes brilliantly blue.

'Me, please,' Mark begged, fighting to release his
seat belt.

'OK. Up we go.' And Nathan swung the youngster
up into his arms and turned to pass him to the steward
who had been taking special care of their little group
on the flight.

'Did you eat an elephant?' the young man teased
Mark as he made his way out of the open exit. 'I'm
sure you weren't this heavy when you came on the
plane. . .'

'You're next, Matthew. Let's get you out of here.'
And Nathan released his son's seat belt while Karen
made certain that she'd gathered all their hand luggage
together.

By the time they reached the bottom of the steps,
Mark was already settled into his wheelchair, and it
was the work of just a few seconds before the four of
them were making their way across the snow-covered
tarmac towards the brightly lit buildings, Mark and
Matthew both trying to catch the falling snowflakes in
their warmly mittened hands.

In no time at all they had been kitted out in all-in-one
suits and boots and transferred to the coach which would
take them to their destination.

'When will we see Father Christmas?' Matthew whispered when he'd beckoned Karen to bend closer. 'Do
you think he got my letter? Does he know we're here?'

'Oh, he must,' Karen reassured him quietly. 'Look
out of the window. That's real Father Christmas
weather, isn't it?'

'Will we see him tonight?' Mark demanded eagerly.

'I don't know,' Karen said honestly because she

couldn't remember the details on their itinerary. 'I wouldn't have thought that he would have his reindeer out in this sort of weather. They're probably inside a stable all warm and dry while Father Christmas is sorting through all the letters he's received.'

Karen felt faintly shy when she looked up and found Nathan's dark eyes fixed on her as she spun the familiar tales to the two boys, but the embarrassment disappeared completely when he smiled his approval of her efforts.

Temporarily out of questions, and a little tired from all the travelling, Mark and Matthew were content to watch the snow-covered scenery go by with only an occasional comment about the appearance of so much snow.

They were still apparently in the middle of nowhere when the coach suddenly slowed down to a halt in the middle of the road.

'Are we there?'

'What's happening?'

The general hubbub died away when their guide called for everyone's attention over the loudspeaker system.

'If you would like to look to your left, you will see some elk just walking away from the front of the coach,' the young woman announced in perfect English.

Karen spared a quick glance at their charges and saw their eyes grow enormous when they saw the size of the animals moving majestically off the side of the road towards a stand of snow-covered trees.

'As you can see,' their guide continued, 'they are very large, with powerful antlers, and they are a protected species in Finland, so these are very good reasons for slowing down to let them move out of the way.'

There was a short burst of general laughter as the coach got under way again and within a few minutes they were entering what appeared to be a small village and drawing up outside the main building of the hotel complex.

Once again Mark and Matthew received preferential treatment and the four of them were soon registered and on their way to their assigned accommodation with the two boys trying to catch snowflakes on their tongues.

'Oh, wow! Look!'

'Dad! It's a log cabin!'

Two excited voices rang out in the darkness as they arrived outside the small wooden structure with a thick covering of snow on the roof.

A light had been switched on beside the front door and a wide circle of gold spilled over the snow in a halo of welcome.

With willing staff to help with the transfer of wheel-chairs and luggage they were soon inside the cosy warmth of their own little cabin.

'That's a welcome sight,' Nathan's husky voice commented approvingly as he went across the room to the stone-built fireplace already filled with crackling logs and began to remove his thick outer clothing.

Mark and Matthew couldn't wait to let Karen help them off with their outerwear. They wanted to go exploring.

'We've found the toilet and a shower and there's a funny room with wooden shelves,' they shouted excitedly.

Karen smiled as she listened to their running commentary on everything they saw while she peeled her own thick clothing off and hung it on one of the wooden pegs driven into the wall.

She turned herself round in a complete circle to inspect the room, admiring the simple decoration and clever use of space and colour.

The walls and roof were entirely composed of wooden logs and the floor was pine, polished to a deep honey shine with brightly coloured rugs positioned at strategic intervals.

Suddenly, she realised that Nathan was standing very still, his eyes fixed on the opposite wall of the cabin.

'What's the matter?' Karen asked as she turned to follow his gaze. 'What have you. . .? Oh. . .' Her breath left her in a silent stream as she recognised what he'd seen.

'Yes. Oh,' he muttered as they both gazed in horrified amazement at the bunk beds built into the wall of the cabin.

At first sight, Karen had thought she was looking at two spacious settees set back against the wall of the cabin, but now she could see that she'd been wrong.

There were two single bunk beds built into the wall several feet above floor level, where the cabin roof sloped towards the apex, and, below them, two double bunks, each covered with bedding in a striking Christmassy red and green pattern.

Karen swallowed.

'I take it this is the combined living room and bed-room,' she said in a thready voice.

'It looks like it.' He hesitated, looking more than a little uncomfortable. 'Would you rather I phoned through to the main building to find out if they can move us into the ordinary hotel accommodation? I'm sure you weren't expecting to find this. . .'

'Oh, wow! Bunk beds!' Mark enthused as he arrived back in the cabin's main room. 'I've always wanted to have a go at sleeping in a bunk bed.'

'Me too,' Matthew echoed. 'And there's a television too. Will it have all foreign programmes?'

'Why don't the two of you settle down for a minute and find out?' Nathan suggested, his professional eye giving each of them the once-over. 'It'll take us a few minutes to get ourselves sorted out in here and then we'll go across to the main building.'

Karen, too, noted their feverish excitement as they fought their way out of their bulky outerwear and piled it around their feet then slid themselves onto the short up-ended logs which served as fireside stools.

As soon as the boys' attention was firmly fixed on trying all the channels, he beckoned Karen over to the tiny kitchenette in the corner of the cabin.

'I'm sorry, but it looks as if we're stuck with the situation,' he began.

'We couldn't possibly move into the main building now,' Karen agreed. 'The boys have set their hearts on this.' She gestured towards the room behind them.

'But what about you? It's hardly right to expect you to share with three males. Shall I see if they can accommodate you in a single room elsewhere?'

'That would defeat the whole object of having the two of us on the trip,' she pointed out. 'You're going to need two pairs of hands to cope with the two of them—especially in strange surroundings and with the two of them so excited.'

'You're quite right,' he conceded. 'If one of them wasn't well in the night, it could end up being a bit of a nightmare trying to cope alone. It could take several minutes before anyone could answer a call for help.'

'Anyway,' Karen continued brightly, ignoring the kaleidoscope of mental images which were bombarding her, 'there's no reason why we shouldn't be able to manage very well. The cabins are compact but there are enough beds for all of us and we can easily organise a rota for the bathroom. . .'

She quickly turned away from him and bent to busily gather up the beautiful rugs scattered over the plain wooden floor. She knew that they would make moving about more difficult with the boys in their wheelchairs but the frantic activity was really no more than camouflage for the sudden heat which had surged into her cheeks.

She had a horrible feeling that if she had still been looking at Nathan when her unruly imagination had insisted on supplying full-colour pictures of his naked body under the shower or even stretched out just inches away from her own he would have been able to tell exactly what she was thinking.

'Karen?' His husky voice drew her eyes back to him. 'Are you certain about this? I never thought about the possibility that it could be a one-room cabin.'

'Don't worry about it, Nathan. We're professional carers and I think we know each other well enough by now that we can put the boys' needs first, rather than the possibility of a little personal embarrassment.'

He was silent for a moment, his eyes watching her intently as if he wanted to look right inside her head. Finally he gave a brief nod and straightened up as he glanced down at his watch.

'We're two hours ahead of Greenwich Mean Time here, aren't we?' he said as he went to adjust the time shown on the slim stainless-steel timepiece strapped to his wrist. 'I think it's time we got the boys ready to go across for the evening meal.'

Almost as soon as the last zip was closed, there was a jingling sound outside the cabin door and a sharp rapping on the solid wood.

Matthew was the first to reach the door and he paused just long enough to ask his father for permission to open it before he pulled it wide.

'Mark! Quick!' he squealed. 'Come and look!'

Karen blinked in confusion and looked across at Nathan who smiled mysteriously as he gestured for her to follow the two boys to the door.

'A sleigh! It's a real sleigh!' Mark breathed ecstatically as his eyes nearly eclipsed his face.

'I think it's come to take us to dinner,' Nathan said seriously. 'Does anyone want to ride in it?'

Between them, he and Karen settled the two boys among the furs and folded their wheelchairs up to travel behind the seats.

'Is everybody ready?' their young driver demanded with a grin. 'Then let's go!' And he gave the reindeer the command to walk.

Nathan and Karen watched for a moment as the sleigh circled around to point in the right direction and they had a wonderful view of the two boys' faces beaming with delight at the novel form of transport.

'We're going to race you,' Matthew taunted in a sing-sing voice as they set off towards the restaurant.

'Not for long,' Nathan called after them. 'Don't eat all the food before we get there.'

He smiled down at Karen and she could see by the warmth in his deep blue eyes exactly how happy he felt.

'I would never have believed the difference in those two boys if I hadn't seen it for myself,' he mused as he put one mittened hand at Karen's back to guide her along the smowy path. 'Seeing them in the sleigh just now, you would hardly know that there was anything wrong with either of them.'

'It's the magic,' Karen murmured, every cell in her body aware that he hadn't taken his hand away once they were walking. Instead, he had moved closer to her so that his arm now slanted protectively across her back, his hand resting easily at her waist as though they always walked like this.

For the few minutes it took them to reach the bright lights of the main building she was perfectly content to let him guide her along the path through the softly drifting flakes of snow.

Mark and Matthew had returned to their wheelchairs once the magical ride was over. Nathan had discussed their special problems openly with the two boys, and had suggested that it would be one way of conserving their energy for more exciting things.

The arrangements at the restaurant were superb, with a choice of traditional Finnish dishes and delicacies, but also dishes showing the influences of Western and Russian cooking.

'I don't believe it!' Nathan laughed. 'We come away to a foreign country and what have these two philistines chosen? Fish and chips!'

'So have you,' Karen pointed out with a cheeky grin.

'You're as bad as they are,' he accused. 'Trout with hollandaise sauce and sauté potatoes is *not* fish and chips!'

The banter back and forth continued throughout the meal, with the boys each taking their turn in the firing line. Towards the end of the meal, Matthew became quiet and a slight frown appeared on his face.

'Are you feeling all right?' Nathan asked quietly under the cover of the noise at the other tables. 'Not feeling too tired?'

'No.' He shook his head. 'It's just. . . Dad, what should Mark and me call her?' He glanced swiftly across at Karen. 'In the hospital she's a nurse, but here. . . She's come to help you look after us but she's not the same.'

When Nathan looked at Karen with one eyebrow raised questioningly, she knew what he was asking and nodded slightly in reply.

'Well, now. That is a bit of a problem.' He put both elbows on the table and linked his hands, his index fingers coming up to tap against his lips as though he was deep in thought. 'Suppose we ask her what she would like you to call her?'

'Well?' Matthew demanded directly, his eyes so exactly like his father's at that moment that Karen was tempted to grin at the uncanny resemblance.

'Have you got any suggestions?' she asked with a smile. 'I have to warn you that I never answer to "Hey, you!".'

'Your name's Karen, isn't it?' Mark said. 'I heard one of the other nurses at the hospital say it.'

'Yes.' Karen smiled at the wary look the two boys shared.

'Would it be all right if we called you Karen, then? Even though you're so old?'

She heard Nathan smother a laugh and had to concentrate hard not to look at him in case she started too.

'Your mum and dad told you that you had to be polite to older people and not use their first names,' she guessed.

'Yes,' he nodded. 'But if you said it was OK. . .?'

'In that case. . .' Karen held her hand out to each boy in turn. 'My name is Karen and I'm very pleased to meet you.'

'That makes it all right, eh, Dad?' Matthew said.

'Quite all right,' he agreed, apparently soberly, but Karen could see the mirth concealed under his thick lashes.

Their waitress came to clear away the debris from their meal and told Mark and Matthew that there was a special entertainment laid on for their younger clients which was just about to begin at the other side of the restaurant.

'A magician!' Their eyes lit up. 'Can we go and watch?'

'Of course you can!' Nathan agreed. 'We'll take you straight over.' He stood up and manoeuvred the first chair away from the table as Karen followed suit with the other.

'Shall I have your coffee waiting at your table when you return?' the pretty, flaxen-haired woman asked.

'Oh.' Karen paused, looking from the two boys to Nathan and back.

'There will be plenty of members of staff to look after the children,' she said helpfully. 'We do this for all the mothers and fathers so they can have a little time without their children at the end of the meal.'

'In that case, I think it's a wonderful idea,' Nathan agreed swiftly, and turned to push Matthew towards a growing hubbub of childish voices before Karen had a chance to tell the young woman that she and Nathan were not Mark and Matthew's parents. At least, he was Matthew's father but she wasn't his wife or the mother of. . . 'Oh, forget it,' she muttered to herself. 'Who cares what she thinks?'

Except. . . Just for a tiny second she had felt a definite thrill at the thought that the waitress had believed Nathan was her husband. . .

Later that evening, Karen was amazed that she'd ever managed to cope with a whole ward full of children after the tussles she and Nathan had gone through to get two small boys to bed.

Partly, the problem had been a simple matter of the two of them being over-tired and over-excited, and when that was added to the novelty of a strange cabin in a strange country with miles of deep snow all around and the prospect of seeing Father Christmas at any moment it was no wonder that they were almost floating off the ceiling.

In spite of all the excitement, there had still been the discipline of the various drugs regimens the two of them were on and the swift check of their vital signs to be taken and noted down.

The two of them had insisted that they wanted to sleep in the top bunks and that they would be climbing up the ladder by themselves.

'Phew!' Karen collapsed onto the edge of one of the lower bunks as Nathan went around the room turning off all but one of the lamps, leaving the cosy cabin bathed in a soft yellow light. 'For a while I thought we were going to have a problem getting them off to sleep, but as soon as their heads touched the pillows they were gone!'

'I don't think we'll hear a sound out of them until the morning,' Nathan commented as he sprawled back into the corner of the same double bunk, his long legs angled across towards the feet she'd tucked up beneath her.

'Did. . .did you want a cup of coffee?' Karen offered, suddenly nervous as she realised the implications of what he'd just said. To all intents and purposes, the two of them were alone in this isolated cabin, sitting together on a double bed in a dimly lit room. . .

'No, thank you,' he mumbled around a jaw-cracking yawn. 'I don't think even coffee stands a chance of keeping me awake tonight.'

'I suppose if we're going to have the energy to keep up with those two tomorrow we ought to be going to bed too. . .I mean. . .' She stumbled to a halt when she realised just how her words had sounded.

'I know what you mean,' Nathan said with a tired chuckle which deteriorated into another yawn. 'Unfortunately I haven't even got the energy to tease you about your *double entendre*, let alone take you up on it. . .'

He dragged himself out of his comfortable corner and reached for her hand to pull her upright.

'You've got just five minutes in the bathroom before I fall asleep on my feet, so get moving, woman.'

Karen grabbed the wash kit and nightwear she'd left ready and set off for the compact bathroom, glancing back once as she reached the doorway to see Nathan crouching in front of the fire to bank it up safely for the night.

Exhaustion worked better than sleeping pills, Karen decided when she woke up the next morning.

She'd slid rapidly under the covers as soon as Nathan had disappeared into the bathroom, with her full-length wrap draped conveniently close in case she needed to grab it in a hurry in the night to tend to one of the boys.

A scowl marred her features when she thought about all the pretty nightdresses she'd left in the drawer at home. Bearing in mind the expected temperatures for this part of Finland at this time of year, she'd decided to bring a sensible pair of brushed-cotton pyjamas. At the time she'd had no idea that Nathan would be anywhere near her when she was wearing the bulky pink monstrosities.

Now she lay in the half-light of an Arctic morning, as warm as toast in her unfashionable nightwear, and realised that she couldn't even remember Nathan returning from the bathroom.

'Good morning, sleepyhead,' his husky voice murmured in the quiet of the cabin, and she lifted her head to look down the length of her bunk towards the second one built against the same wall.

'Good morning,' she mumbled when she realised that he had positioned himself to sleep at the other end of his bunk so that their feet were mere inches apart.

With his head propped up against the rumpled pillow on the arms folded casually beneath it, he could have been lying there looking at her for ages without her knowing. . .

In the soft glow of the night light he must have left on for the boys' sake, his deep blue eyes were brilliant under half-lowered lids in a face shadowed by the dark blond stubble of his emerging beard.

He looked as lazy as a sleepy mountain lion, and just as potentially lethal to an unwary companion.

As her own eyes returned to his after a leisurely perusal of his naked arms, the muscles outlined in gold and bronze in the soft light, she saw one eyebrow arch and blushed uncomfortably, dragging her gaze away from his quizzical expression.

'You remind me of a rabbit,' he murmured, with unmistakable laughter in his husky voice.

'A rabbit?' she squeaked in disgust, only just remembering in time to keep her voice low so that she didn't disturb the boys.

'Yes.' His eyes swept across her and she clenched her fingers over the edge of the brightly coloured bedclothes, knowing what he could see, but unable to do anything about the untidy tangle of her usually neat hair or her sleep-warmed cheeks.

'You look all pink and fluffy and cuddly in your. . . What *are* you wearing, for heaven's sake?'

'Pyjamas,' she said grumpily. 'Winceyette pyjamas, to be exact, because I didn't know the heating was going to be so efficient in such a remote place.'

There were several moments of silence while he absorbed the information and she glared at him, daring him to say anything more about it.

Finally, he seemed to have the threatening laughter under control. 'Would you like to go to the bathroom first?' he offered politely.

Karen thought about Nathan lying there watching her while she struggled into her wrap without letting him see the true extent of the gruesomeness of the pyjamas, and couldn't bear it. If he was in the bathroom she would have the chance to hide them away before he returned.

'No. That's all right,' she said hastily. 'It's your turn to go first this time.'

'Ah.' He pursed his mouth. 'That could cause a bit of a problem.'

'Why?'

'Because I *don't* wear pink pyjamas. . .'

Her heart beat normally several times before she understood what he meant, and then it stopped dead for a second.

'Oh!' she gasped as her eyes flew to the long, lean shape of him hidden by the bedclothes, and her face flamed as she imagined his naked body stretched out just out of reach.

He stirred under her gaze and raised one knee as if to make a concealing tent of the bright cotton fabric and she whipped her head away to stare at the pine logs which made up the cabin wall just inches away from her nose when he grasped the covers in one hand to lift them aside.

Her ears straining to hear the rustle of the bedclothes, she waited until everything was silent before she chanced a quick glance over her shoulder to see if it was safe to reach for her wrap.

He hadn't gone yet and suddenly she found that she couldn't drag her eyes away from him.

As her eyes focused in the soft light she saw him standing beside his bed dressed only in a pair of dark underpants as he reached for his wash kit and clothes.

She must have made a sound because his head came up to catch her eyes on him.

'And I thought I could trust you not to peep!' he teased in a whisper as he straightened up to his full height and she saw for the first time that his tall, broad-shouldered body was every bit as magnificent as she'd imagined.

Suddenly realising that she was blatantly staring, Karen screwed her eyes up tight and pulled the covers right up to her eyebrows to hide her blushes, listening to the soft sounds as he walked past her bunk barefoot, his chuckle taunting her long after he'd left the room.

'What are we going to do today?' Mark demanded. 'When will we see Father Christmas?'

Matthew, too, was full of electric impatience as he was helped into his all-in-one suit ready to go across to the restaurant.

'Well,' Nathan began, 'I thought as soon as we'd had breakfast we could see if we could find the post office.'

Karen nearly laughed aloud when she saw their little faces fall at the apparently boring suggestion.

'Father Christmas's post office,' Nathan continued, to the accompaniment of squeals of delight.

'Will he be there?' Matthew's cheeks were pink with excitement. 'Will Father Christmas be there. . .and his elves?'

'I've no idea. We'll just have to wait and see—'

His words were interrupted by the sound of sleigh bells outside and the boys knew that their own personal 'taxi' had arrived to take them across to the restaurant.

As she shut the door behind them, Karen wished she could have gone with them instead of having to walk across with Nathan. What was she supposed to say to him after ogling him like that this morning?

'Have you brought any money with you?' His husky voice startled her out of her thoughts.

'Money?' she repeated, wondering how much of the conversation she had missed.

'To visit the post office,' he explained patiently. 'Because they're so strict about not allowing this place to become over-commercialised, it's the only place you can buy gifts and souvenirs.'

Karen breathed a silent sigh of relief that the ice had been broken between them and was able to hold up her end of the conversation quite easily until they joined their two young companions.

'We showed Maritta how to unfold the wheelchairs,' they announced proudly when they met Karen and

Nathan in the entrance hall. 'She said we can meet her
brothers today.'

They were chattering nineteen to the dozen over their
shoulders as they were pushed through to the restaurant
and Karen exchanged a smiling glance with Nathan.

'I'm so glad we were able to sort everything out in
time for the trip,' she murmured. 'It's done the two of
them so much good just being here. . .'

'And me too,' Nathan admitted with a wry smile.
'I'd allowed myself to get so wrapped up in the fact of
Matthew's illness and the successes and failures of his
treatment that I'd almost forgotten about the child.'

Karen frowned in concentration as she followed his
quiet words, grateful for the fact that the two lads were
occupied with their own conversation for the moment.
She had a feeling that this was very important to Nathan
and was an insight into the way this essentially private
man thought and felt.

It wasn't until after they'd finished their breakfast
and the boys were getting ready to go back out into the
snowy wonderland again that Nathan returned to what
he was saying before.

'You know, Karen,' he said, with a new light of
determination in his eyes, 'this trip has reminded me
that for all his amazing stoicism over his treatment
Matthew's a six-year-old boy who still believes in
magic and happy-ever-after, and I'm going to do my
best to see that he gets it.'

CHAPTER SEVEN

'PUSH me! Harder!' Mark demanded, then squealed in delight when he began to slide down the gentle slope.

'My turn!' Matthew was ready and waiting to be sent after him.

'Who would have thought that two overgrown tea-trays could give so much pleasure?' Karen said with a happy laugh.

'The trouble is, it's a bit like a puppy with a stick,' Nathan groaned as he straightened up from his latest effort. 'The more times you throw the thing, the more times he brings it back for another go.'

'Except, in this case, we have to do the retrieving as well,' Karen reminded him as they made their way down to the bottom of the slope where the boys had come to rest.

It was the work of a minute to loop a rope through the stout handles of each toboggan and begin to tow them back up the slope again.

They had nearly reached the top when Karen heard the now familiar sound of the deep square bell worn by a reindeer and glanced across towards the track between the trees.

'Mark! Matthew! Quick!'

As she spoke, she bent to lift Mark up so that he could see what had caught her eye.

'Who can you see?'

She pointed towards the reindeer-drawn sleigh which they could see travelling almost parallel to them

116

between the snow-covered trunks and branches of the trees.

Nathan had swung Matthew to his feet and was crouching with one arm around his shoulders as he pointed towards the red-suited figure who began waving in their direction.

'It's Father Christmas!' Mark whispered in awe, his grey eyes growing round with amazement. 'He's really here!' he said in a stronger voice. 'Matthew! It's Father Christmas! Look!' His voice rose higher and higher with excitement, and when the familiar red arm waved again the two boys began waving wildly in reply.

Karen was just conscious of the click and whirr as Nathan wielded the camera again and was grateful that he was the one in charge of recording the trip for Mark's parents. She had been so caught up in the boys' excitement that she hadn't given a thought to catching the moment on film.

'Where was he going?' Mark wanted to know.

'Why didn't he stop?' Matthew demanded, his expression growing quite distraught.

'He's probably on his way to check up on the elves,' Karen suggested quickly. 'It's Christmas Eve today, and in Finland that's the day that everyone gets their presents, so he's very busy.'

'But he *does* know we've come to see him, doesn't he? He won't forget?'

'Of course he knows you've come!' Nathan reassured them seriously. 'He waved to you on his way past!'

'And we will see him?' Matthew's dark blue eyes, so like his father's, were travelling from one adult to the other as if he needed reassurance from both of them to calm his fears.

'Yes. You will see him. In fact you'll even be able to speak to him,' Nathan said. 'I promise.'

Karen swallowed to clear the tears thickening her throat as she saw the utter trust on the two boys' faces.

'Right, now. I think it's time we sent a grown-up down this slope,' she proposed, looking pointedly at Nathan, and was rewarded by shouts of glee at the outrageous prospect of sending Matthew's father down the slope.

'Come on, Dad. Sit on it,' Matthew ordered. 'Mark and me are going to give you a push.'

Nathan's expression promised retribution when he pretended to glare up at Karen, but he folded his long legs up and tucked his knees under his chin with an air of long-suffering as he sat on the bright red plastic toboggan.

'Ready? Steady? Go!' Karen chanted as she helped them to send him on his way amidst a chorus of laughter, all their worries forgotten in the fun.

Their trip in the sleigh after breakfast had been a great success, the pony's harness jingling with every step as he'd shaken the bells attached to it.

Nathan had started singing the Christmas song about the one-horse open sleigh, his husky voice echoing back to them from the snowy slopes until all of them had joined in as the runners slid easily over the packed snow in the strange Arctic half-light.

Everywhere they'd looked there had been trees and more trees, each one covered with a heavy burden of snow, enough to weigh the branches down so that when Mark had reached out to touch one with his hand as they slid past he'd disturbed a whole shower onto Nathan's lap.

'Hey! Monster!' Nathan had roared as he'd heaved

the snow out of the sleigh and wiped his face. 'That was cold! Just you wait!' he'd threatened with a terrible scowl. 'I'll get you for that!'

Mark and Matthew had gone off into gales of laughter, totally unworried by the faces Nathan was pulling.

At lunchtime they settled themselves aboard long sleighs which were pulled by a team of husky dogs. The seven dogs pulled them swiftly through the silent wilderness, along tracks deep into the forest, to a nomads' camp where they would meet up with other hotel guests to have lunch cooked out in the open air.

In their all-in-one suits and boots they were all as warm as toast but when they reached the camp Matthew spotted something special.

'Look, Dad. Over there. It's a tepee!' He pointed out the tall conical shape, constructed in the same way as those in North America, with animal skins over long poles, but in this case one side had been left open and a small log fire had been lit within its shelter.

'There are seats in there,' Mark said as they stopped nearby. 'Fat pieces of logs, like the ones in our cabin. Can we go in there?'

One of the young helpers standing by the huge cauldrons of soup and stew bubbling over the open fire had obviously heard their piping voices because he turned with a smile.

'Of course you can go in the *kota*. Warm yourselves by the *nuotio*.'

While Nathan and Karen settled the two boys on the upturned logs which fascinated them so much, the young man filled cups with steaming soup which he carried in to them. He spent several minutes with them, teaching them to repeat the Lappish words for tepee and campfire, and promising to bring them their stew as soon as they were ready for it.

'Soup for you too?' Nathan asked Karen.

'Please. I'm starving! I must have used up all my energy pushing you down the slope on the toboggan!'

He pulled another gruesome face at her, which sent the two boys off into gales of laughter again.

'Behave, Doctor,' she said sternly when he returned with two steaming cups. 'I won't have you ruining these boys' digestive systems.'

'Yes, Staff Nurse. I'm sorry.' He tried to look suitably penitent but ended up laughing too, his face becoming relaxed as the tension which usually gripped him melted away.

Karen found her eyes straying from Nathan to his son and back again and a nameless longing filled her.

When Gareth had let her down so cruelly, she had sworn that she wouldn't allow anyone to get close enough to her to care; close enough to hurt her.

Now, for the first time in years, someone had found their way behind the shield she'd erected around her feelings, and she found herself wondering what it would be like to have a family of her own—a husband and son to love her and for her to love in return.

It was a sharp little voice at the back of her conscience which forced her to admit the truth to herself. She didn't just want *anyone*. She wanted *them* as her family—to be married to Nathan and for Matthew to be their son.

Karen had forgotten Nathan's threats completely until they returned to their cabin after lunch.

The sleigh had deposited them outside their cabin and she had just set Mark down on the bottom step to help him off with his boots when Nathan called her.

'Karen?'

'Yes?' She turned towards the sound of his voice and a large soft snowball exploded on her shoulder, showering her with snow.

'Oof! That's cold!' Karen shrieked in shock.

'Dad!' Matthew sounded scandalised, then squealed when it was his turn to be bombarded.

'And you!' Nathan growled, making sure no one felt left out when he tossed one carefully at Mark to hit him fair and square in the middle of his chest.

'Right, you two. Help me,' Karen called. 'This is war. . .!' And she gathered up a double handful of snow and aimed it wildly at Nathan while Mark leant forward to gather snow from the pile by the steps.

Nathan managed to duck her first missile easily, but once the two boys joined in and all three of them were throwing snow at him as fast as they could he soon ended up looking like a walking snowman.

'Not fair!' he shouted as he charged straight at Karen with a snowball clutched in each hand and she screamed in delicious fear as she whirled and tried to run.

Unfortunately, she'd forgotten how deep the snow was and how cumbersome the boots were and she'd hardly gone half a dozen paces round the corner of the cabin before Nathan caught up with her just as she threw a despairing glance over her shoulder. Before she could do anything to save herself, she was tumbling into a snowdrift, her hat flying off to release her hair, which lay like a fine-spun gold halo around her head.

'No!' she squealed as she wriggled under his weight, expecting to get both handfuls of snow in her face at any second.

Suddenly, she realised that Nathan had grown still

and she opened one eye warily to find him staring down at her with an arrested look on his face.

'Nathan?' she murmured uncertainly when she realised that he wasn't moving. 'What's the matter. . .?'

Before she realised what was happening, his lips had stolen the words away, and her breath with them.

She'd never thought that a kiss could be hot and cold at the same time, but this one was. His lips were cold from the sub-zero temperatures and the snow they'd been throwing at him, but his tongue, when it touched her own cold lips in a blatant demand for entry, was as hot as a burning brand.

'Dad?'

Matthew's little voice reached Karen through the fog of desire which had enveloped her out of nowhere.

Suddenly, Nathan's mouth was torn away from her and he was gazing down into her face with a shocked expression in his eyes.

A diminutive pair of boots crunched laboriously to a halt beside them.

'What are you doing?' he asked with a typical six-year-old's directness.

What *were* they doing? Karen thought in horror. They had two young boys in their care and they'd left one of them sitting at the bottom of a flight of snowy steps hardly able to get himself up them alone. How could they have allowed themselves to roll about in the snow, kissing as though. . .?

'I was going to teach Karen how to make a snow angel,' Nathan said hoarsely, his voice sounding as if it was emerging over gravel.

'Me too!' Matthew demanded as the strangely speculative expression disappeared from his little face. 'Teach me and Mark too!'

For just a second, while Matthew returned to Mark to tell him what was happening, Nathan gazed down into Karen's stunned face, his pupils so widely dilated that his dark blue eyes looked nearly black.

With a muttered oath, he rolled away from her and sat up, his wrists draped over his bent knees as he stared out across the snowy clearing.

Karen found herself holding her breath, waiting for him to say something, but he just shook his head as he sighed deeply then offered her a hand to get out of the snow.

With a sudden surge of self-consciousness Karen realised that she was still lying spread-eagled in the snow exactly the way he had left her after their kiss.

Ignoring his offer of help, she struggled up, surprised to find that there was still a thick layer of snow underneath her. The temperature of that kiss should have turned it to steam, she thought with a weak attempt at humour.

'Come on, Dad!' Matthew prompted as he stuck his head back round the corner. 'Me and Mark are waiting to make angels!'

With a final smouldering glance at Karen, he pushed himself to his feet and cleared his throat.

'Instructions for making snow angels coming up!' he announced as he went to join the two of them.

For a minute, Karen stayed where she was, listening to the laughter coming from round the corner of the cabin as she tried to come to terms with what had just happened between Nathan and herself.

'Karen? Come on. . .you're missing all the fun!' Matthew's childish voice intruded.

'That's what you think!' she muttered as she retrieved her hat and pulled it down over her bedraggled hair.

She stumbled through the small drift, her knees not quite working as well as they should in the aftermath of the heat.

She rounded the corner of the cabin to find the three of them laid out flat on their backs at intervals on a large unmarked area of snow.

'Your space is over next to Dad,' Matthew directed. 'First, you've got to get down very carefully so you don't make any marks.'

Karen made her way reluctantly towards Nathan, knowing from his raised head that he was watching her.

'She's ready, Dad. What do we do now?'

'Slowly slide your arms up and down in the snow as if you're flapping your wings like a bird.' Nathan raised his hands from their position at his sides until they were above the level of his shoulders, then slid them down again to demonstrate what he meant, but the whole time Karen could feel his eyes on her, and she had to fight not to turn her head to meet their gaze.

'Now what?' Mark's voice sounded from the other side of Matthew.

'Now do the same with your legs,' Nathan's husky voice directed, and Karen felt her face flame as she remembered the way she'd parted her own legs when he'd been on top of her, his hips meshing perfectly into the space she'd created for him. . .

'Now you get up very carefully so you don't spoil it. If you wait a minute, I'll help you. . .'

Karen heard him getting up and knew that it would be safe to look his way at last, relishing the chance to watch him as he gently took the boys' hands in turn and pulled them to their feet.

'Come and see, Karen,' Matthew demanded, beckoning her over when she managed to extricate herself from the pattern she'd made. 'We've made a whole family of angels in the snow—a daddy, a mummy and two little angels. Look!'

He was quite right.

The sweeping movements of their arms had made shapes that looked just like angels' wings, and the three different sizes looked like the perfect family unit.

'Two little angels?' she scoffed in a voice made husky by emotion. 'Two little imps is more like it. . .' And she brushed the snow off them and chased them inside the cabin to have a warm drink.

It was about an hour later, when the four of them were just settling themselves into the sleigh which had apparently come to take them across to the main hotel complex, that they heard the sound of a reindeer bell again.

This time it was Mark who saw the red-suited figure in the sleigh first.

'There he is!' he shouted. 'Look, Matthew, he's going that way.'

To their delight he waved to them again, this time beckoning them to follow his sleigh.

The two boys were so excited they were nearly bouncing out of their seats as the driver directed their sleigh in the same direction. Mark and Matthew were craning their necks out at opposite sides to keep the splash of red in sight, worried that this might be their only chance to catch up with their elusive quarry.

'There!' Karen exclaimed as they rounded a curve in the track between the closely packed trees. 'There's a cabin up ahead.'

As they drew closer, they could see the red-clad figure getting out of the sleigh and going into the cabin, the sleigh being led round to the back of the cabin by the younger, brightly dressed figure of one of the elves.

The driver halted right in front of the cabin and pointed to the word carved into a piece of wood above the door.

'Joulupukki,' he read, and the two boys immediately repeated the word, having learnt it only this morning.

'Did someone say my name?' a voice said from inside the cabin, and a door opened to reveal Father Christmas himself.

'Welcome,' he said with a smile, his cheeks as rosy as polished red apples above his curly white beard. 'Come in, come in.' He turned and led the way into the little cabin.

For a moment, Mark and Matthew were so overawed that they just stood watching him, until Nathan gave them a nudge, one hand reaching for the camera slung on a strap around his neck.

'Tell me,' the old gentleman prompted once they were all shut inside the cosy cabin. 'Have you come a long way to see me?'

'From England,' Mark supplied in a shaky voice. 'In an aeroplane.'

'We sent you letters to let you know we were coming,' Matthew added.

'Ah!' He smiled and nodded. 'And what are your names?'

'I'm Mark.'

'And I'm Matthew.'

'Ah, yes. Mark and Matthew.' The blue eyes looked from one to the other then he turned to a small table beside him and picked up two pieces of paper. 'Mark Hooper and Matthew Beckett,' he said importantly, and beckoned them closer as he sat down on a wooden chair beside a large decorated Christmas tree. 'I have your letters here. See.'

When she saw the expressions of amazement on their young faces as they each recognised the letters they had written and posted back in England, Karen had to glance across at Nathan to share her pleasure with him.

As if he knew what she was feeling, Nathan's hand reached for hers and held it tightly while they listened to the conversation between the gentle old man and the two enraptured children.

In no time at all he had put them at their ease and within minutes they were confiding in him about their illnesses and the charity which had granted them their wishes, just as if he were a favourite grandfather.

Mark even lifted his hat off to display the angry scars which remained from the attempts to remove the glioma which was slowly killing him, the livid tracks of the surgeon's knife clearly visible through the baby-fine red-gold hair.

'Such brave boys,' the old man murmured in his accented English as he gently helped Mark to pull the hat down to cover the evidence again.

The progression of his illness meant that Mark had begun to tire very easily and he was gradually losing the use of his legs, but when he began to sway it was Father Christmas who lifted him up and sat him on a red-clad knee then put his other arm around Matthew's shoulders to draw him into the circle and give them both a hug.

He glanced up swiftly at Nathan and Karen and they could see the moisture that had gathered in his bright blue eyes when he nodded to Nathan to take his photographs.

'Now, then,' he said with a newly gruff voice,

directing his words to the two adults. 'Have they been good boys while they have been visiting my country? Have they been enjoying themselves?'

'Of course,' Karen said with a tremulous smile, so grateful for the gentle patience he was showing to the two little boys. 'They've had a ride in a sleigh and helped to feed the reindeer.'

'And gone tobogganing and had a snowball fight,' Nathan added.

'Good. Very good. And will they be helping to decorate the Christmas tree at the hotel this evening?' he prompted, looking back down at the two of them.

'Yes!' Mark replied eagerly. 'And a little one in our cabin.'

'Our cabin's made out of trees, just like yours,' Matthew volunteered. 'And it's got a fireplace with a big chimney in the corner, too.'

'Good.' He nodded sagely. 'A country so full of snow is fine for boys to play in, but you must have a good cabin to stay warm.'

He looked across at Nathan and Karen and raised a snowy white eyebrow.

'Could you perhaps help me for a minute?' He tightened his arms around the boys' shoulders. 'I need someone to fetch the two parcels from under the tree over there.'

'These ones?' Nathan pointed to two large square boxes wrapped in Christmas paper as he crouched beside the tree.

'Just so.'

Nathan handed one up to Karen with a smile and stood with the other.

'Will you bring them over here so these fine boys can tell me what names are written on them?'

'This one says Matthew,' Matthew announced in surprise.

'And this one says Mark.' Mark's voice rose to a squeak when he recognised his own name.

The two of them beamed their delight at each other then at everyone in sight.

'Well, if they have *your* names on them, that must mean that my elves want you to have them.'

'Thank you,' Matthew breathed, almost speechless with pleasure as he gazed from Father Christmas to the box and back again.

'Oh, Father Christmas. . .' Mark's little chin was wobbling as he gazed at the large box Karen was holding for him. 'This is my very best Christmas, ever. . .' And he reached up to plant a childish kiss full of love on the old man's cheek.

'Well, boys. . .' He paused a second to clear his throat as he was visibly overcome with emotion. 'I will be seeing you again this evening when you have finished decorating the big tree for me. Now, take your presents back to your cabin to open them. In Lapland we don't make you wait for Christmas Day!' There was a twinkle in his eyes again as Karen helped Mark off his knee and he patted Matthew on the shoulder.

'*Näkemiin* . . . Goodbye,' he said as he got up from his seat to follow them to the cabin door.

'*Näkemiin*, Joulupukki,' the two boys chorused in reply, then suddenly remembered the Lappish phrase they had been practising ever since their waitress, Maritta, had taught them it. '*Kiitos* . . . Thank you.'

'I thank *you* for coming all the way from England to see me,' he said with a smile.

He stood watching while Nathan carried Mark down

the steps and settled him into his seat in the sleigh and Karen helped Matthew into his.

While they'd been in the cabin, it had started to snow again, the softly drifting flakes lending everything a magical air.

They all laughed when neither boy wanted to let go of his parcel for a second, each clutching it tightly on his lap as they waved and called, '*Näkemiin*,' one last time before the sleigh rounded the corner and the cabin and its famous occupant disappeared from sight.

It was nearly dark when they reached their own little cabin again and the two boys were in a fever of excitement to get inside and see what was inside their parcels.

At first, they'd wanted to open them straight away in the sleigh, but with Nathan and Karen's combined persuasion—they had pointed out the possibility of dropping the present from the moving sleigh or of dropping litter as they tore the wrappings away—they had finally agreed to wait.

'Come on, Mark. Hurry up,' Matthew shouted excitedly as he clambered out of the sleigh, hampered by the large package which he refused to relinquish for a second. 'Let's get inside and open them up,' he called as he stomped his way carefully up the snowy steps to the diminutive porch in his big warm boots, guided by the glowing light beside the wooden door.

'Wait for me. . .I'm coming,' Mark called back as his mittened hands fumbled with the slippery parcel.

He reached the bottom step and looked up at Matthew as Karen knelt by the front door helping him to remove his snowy boots.

'Mark, wait for me to help you,' Nathan called as he

rounded the back of the sleigh and thanked their driver, but Mark obviously couldn't bear to wait.

'Don't start without me,' he pleaded as he tried to hurry up steps covered with a fresh layer of snow.

Suddenly, the disaster happened. Whether he slid on the snow or whether his legs simply refused to carry him didn't matter. The result was just as traumatic as he somersaulted off the steps to land with a thud.

'Mark!'

Karen's heart was in her mouth as she saw his little body lying so still. Every muscle was tensed to rush to help him but she had Matthew to take care of too.

'Is he all right?' she called as she swept the sobbing six-year-old into her arms and fought her way to her feet.

Nathan flicked her a quick glance as he knelt beside the still form in the snow, his eyes filled with dark despair that he hadn't reached the youngster in time.

'Can you get the door open and the lights on?' he directed. 'I need more light to check him over before I move him.'

'Come on, Matthew,' Karen said as she turned towards the door, her arms cradling him tightly for comfort. 'We've got a job to do for your dad so he can look after Mark.'

She kept up a soothing chatter as she switched on all the lights which would strengthen the amount pouring out of the front windows and across the strangely silent little boy.

The bright colours of his all-in-one suit looked terribly garish under the artificial light—or was it the horror of the situation which made them seem that way? she wondered.

'Look, Matthew,' she said as she turned his face

towards the window. 'Daddy's picking Mark up to bring him in the cabin.'

'Is he all right? Is Mark all right?' His little face was streaked with tears of fear for his friend, all the healthy colour the past few days had put in his cheeks leached out by the shock.

'We'll ask him in just a minute,' she promised. 'Can you hold the door open for him and shut it when they come inside?'

Pleased to have a job to do, he left his position at the window to take charge of the door.

'Karen?' Nathan called as he carried his little burden in. 'Can you get my. . .? Ah! Well anticipated. . .' He smiled briefly at her when he saw that she'd already retrieved his medical bag and had put it at the end of one of the double bunks.

'Mark? I'm going to take your suit off. Tell me if you hurt anywhere.' Nathan began to undo the fasteners down the front of the padded all-in-one garment and Karen reached across to help him.

She had been so relieved when Nathan had started speaking to Mark. At least her worst fear hadn't come true. Now it just remained to find out exactly how much damage the fall had done.

'Is he alive?' Matthew whispered in a quivering voice. 'Has he hurt his head?'

'Yes, sweetheart,' Karen said, smiling at him over her shoulder and putting as much reassurance into her voice as she could. 'Mark's alive and he's awake. We're just taking his outside clothes off so your dad can check him over for bumps and bruises.'

As soon as she'd done as much as she could to help, she held out one arm to Matthew who burrowed against her side for comfort like a frightened animal.

At last, Nathan clicked off the light he'd been using to check Mark's eye reflexes and sat up with a muted sigh of relief.

'No obvious damage,' he reported. 'I don't think he even lost consciousness. I think he was just a little stunned by the suddenness of the fall.'

'He didn't hit his head?' Karen demanded quietly.

The words were commonplace enough that Matthew wouldn't understand the significance of them, but she knew that tumours such as the one invading Mark's brain were highly vascularised and so were very susceptible to lethal bleeding if they sustained a heavy blow.

'It looks as if his head was so well padded by his hat that it hardly noticed that he'd tried to bounce on it!'

Matthew's chuckle of relief was interrupted by Mark's sudden wail.

'I've lost it,' he sobbed broken-heartedly as tears trickled slowly out of his desolate grey eyes. 'I lost my present from Father Christmas. . .'

For a few seconds he cried inconsolably and Karen's heart sank into her boots.

'Oh, sweetheart,' she began as Nathan straightened up from his position on the side of the double bunk and walked swiftly across the room towards the front door.

Within seconds, he was back—long before Karen had managed to get Mark to listen to her.

'Mark!' Matthew squealed, almost in his friend's ear. 'Look what my dad's got.'

One tear-filled eye opened, swiftly followed by the other when he saw the large, brightly coloured parcel suspended over the top of him.

'You found it,' he breathed, reaching up tentatively to touch it, as if he wasn't certain he could believe his own eyes, then pulling it down awkwardly onto his chest to hug it convulsively. 'Thank you,' he said through a second bout of tears. 'Thank you very much.'

CHAPTER EIGHT

THE present-opening ceremony was delayed just long enough for everyone to take off their outside clothing and for Karen to make them all a hot chocolate drink in the kitchenette.

'Is everyone ready?' Nathan demanded as he positioned himself with the camera. 'I think it's time to see what's in those enormous parcels.'

'Do you want to open them one at a time, or both together?' Karen asked, and the two boys looked at each other for a second.

'Together. . .!'

'Both together. . .!' they said in unison with big grins on their faces, and their little hands began tearing at the bright, shiny wrappings.

'Look!'

'Oh, wow!'

The pictures on the outside of the boxes they'd uncovered were enough to tell the two of them what was inside.

'Computer games!'

'It's just like the one in hospital!'

With one child at each end of the wide double bunk there was plenty of room for them to open up the boxes and explore the contents while Nathan and Karen took the empty mugs across to the kitchenette to wash up and tidy away.

'The only difficulty now is going to be getting them

away from their new possessions long enough to eat and sleep,' Nathan joked.

'Well, Father Christmas couldn't have given them anything they'd have enjoyed more.' She smiled wryly. 'It's going to sound like intergalactic warfare in here when they get them going.'

'In the meantime,' Nathan began as he glanced first at his watch, then at the two boys to make sure they were both fully occupied, 'we've got a few minutes' grace to decide what to do about Mark.'

'In what way?' Karen folded the teatowel over the pine rail.

'Whether to take him over to the main part of the hotel complex to help decorate the tree,' he murmured, keeping his voice low enough so that the youngsters wouldn't hear.

'Could we adopt a ''see how he goes'' policy?' Karen suggested. 'It would be a shame to make both boys stay in the cabin and miss all the fun, then find out that there was nothing wrong with him. There will be two of us keeping an eye on him, and we can always bring him back here if he shows any adverse signs or begins to flag a bit.'

'All right, all right! I give in!' Nathan grinned as he held both hands up in surrender. 'We'll take them over to help decorate the tree.'

When the four of them arrived over at the main log cabin, the tree had just been brought in and set up in a corner of the room.

'You can smell it as soon as you come in,' Karen said as she drew in a lungful of fresh pine. 'It's as if they've brought the outdoors inside.'

'Especially when it mixes with the smell of the burn-

ing logs from the fire,' Nathan agreed, sidestepping
to avoid a collision with a tiny tearaway who was
obviously over-excited already.

'Where did all these children come from?' Karen said
in amazement. 'I didn't realise there were quite so many
on the complex.'

'They must all have been taking part in different
activities when we were over here before. Decorating
the Christmas tree might be the first thing that all of
them have wanted to do at the same time.'

'That, and seeing Father Christmas after dinner,' she
reminded him. 'If you remember from the itinerary,
tonight the adults get presents too!'

Nathan laughed. 'You're a bigger kid than they are!'

'Dad?' Matthew was tugging at his elbow. 'We got
a problem.'

'Have we?' Nathan crouched down so that they were
on a level. 'Tell me about this problem.'

'Well, me and Mark want to help put the things on
the tree but we can't get close enough to do it in our
wheelchairs and we're not tall enough to reach from
the floor.'

'I see.' Nathan put on his most serious consultant's
face as though he was thinking deeply about it. 'So.
Have either of you come up with a solution to the
problem?'

'We-e-ell. . .' Mark drew the word out into at least
three syllables. '*You've* got very long legs,' he observed.

'But you can't borrow them because they're attached
to me,' he pointed out with a pained expression which
made them laugh.

'But if you lifted us up?' Matthew suggested hopefully. 'Then we could borrow them without you taking
them off. . .'

'Sounds like a good plan,' Nathan agreed as he straightened up again. 'Let's try it.'

He and Karen pushed the wheelchairs over to the side of the room so that they wouldn't be in the way then Nathan crouched down in front of Mark's chair.

'Karen, will you steady him while he climbs on my shoulders?' he directed, and she hurried round to lend a hand.

'What about me?' Matthew said plaintively as his father straightened up and Mark was enthralled by his first look at the world from seven feet up in the air.

'Well, I'm not as tall as your dad, but I can certainly give you a piggyback until it's your turn for the highest seat in the house,' Karen volunteered with a smile.

The next hour or so was full of fun and laughter as the tree was decked out in tinsel and baubles galore. Karen was particularly impressed with some brightly painted carved wooden ornaments which swung on fine cords from the tips of the branches.

'They look handmade,' she commented, tightening her hold on Mark while she got him to hold one up to show it to Nathan. 'There are reindeer and sleighs and stars and Christmas trees. . .'

'And Father Christmas,' Matthew pointed out from his perch on his father's shoulders.

Soon the staff were clearing away the last of the boxes which had contained the decorations and while everyone held their breath the main lights were turned off and the lights on the tree switched on for the first time to the sound of cheers and applause.

'Oh, wow,' Matthew breathed.

'It's beautiful,' Mark agreed.

'Of course it's beautiful,' Nathan said. 'After all, we helped to decorate it!'

The main lights came back on again then, dispelling a little of the magic in favour of practicalities as the staff announced that Christmas dinner was ready.

Karen bit back a groan as Mark slid off her back and into his chair. She was going to be stiff tomorrow after carrying the two of them round in relays for the last hour—but it had been well worth it to help them take part in the fun.

As the meal progressed, there was a palpable air of excitement in the room the closer it got to nine o'clock.

Even Nathan seemed to be infected with it, his face wreathed in smiles as he teased and joked with the boys, at times seeming hardly any older than they were.

Finally, the beautiful meal ended and everyone went through to sit around the tree.

They'd only been sitting for a few minutes when one of the children who'd been standing by the window looking out at the freshly falling snow squealed in excitement.

'He's coming! Father Christmas is coming!'

There were several seconds of complete silence as the words registered and into the silence came the sound of a reindeer bell drawing steadily closer.

Mark and Matthew could hardly sit still. In spite of the fact that they had already spoken to Father Christmas today, their eyes were glowing at the prospect of seeing him again.

Karen was so pleased that their trip was turning out to be such a success.

It hardly seemed possible that these were the same two boys who had lain in hospital beds such a short while ago, one undergoing chemotherapy to try to control his acute leukaemia, the other one coping manfully with his progressive disability but so depressed because his parents' injuries would prevent him from taking the trip he'd set his heart on.

In family groups, everyone took their turn to speak to Father Christmas and receive a gift from him, the adults just as enchanted by the special magic of the event and the man as their children.

When it was Nathan, Karen and the boys' turn to go forward, the kindly old man had a special word for Mark as he handed him a small parcel.

'This is my gift to you, Mark, but I need to ask you a question. Will you do a very important job for me, young man?' he asked, his bright blue eyes very serious. 'I have here a present for your mother and father but you have told me that they are in the hospital.'

'Yes. A car smashed into them and they got broken bones.'

'Well, I don't want them to have to wait until they go home to have a present from me, so I would like you to deliver it for me, personally. Will you do this?'

'Yes,' Mark agreed with awe in his voice, his big grey eyes shining. 'I promise.'

'That is good. Very good.' The bright blue eyes sparkled as he put two small parcels onto Mark's lap. 'Take care of them, and take care of yourself. I am very honoured to have met you.' He slid one gnarled hand very gently over the brightly coloured hat which covered the evidence of Mark's illness. Karen saw the brief sadness in his eyes which no smile could cover, and saw, too, the deliberate effort he made to put it behind him before he continued.

'Now you, Matthew.' He turned the warmth of his smile on the younger boy who had been watching the events with wide eyes. 'This is a special present for you. When you look at it when you are back in England,

I hope you will remember coming to see me and perhaps you will remember too that sometimes wishes *do* come true.'

The little gifts he gave to Nathan and Karen were accompanied with a simple, 'God bless you and remind you to be brave and keep hoping.'

When all the gifts had been given and his sack was empty, he stood in the doorway to wave goodbye to all of them, the lights picking out the swirling flakes of snow behind him against the darkness of the night.

'Now, you know that I must leave you to help my elves load up my sleigh. Then my reindeer and I must go around the world to deliver presents to all the other people before they wake up in the morning. Goodbye . . .*Näkemiin!*' And with a final wave he turned and climbed into the empty sleigh and drove away into the darkness.

As if someone had switched their power off, suddenly the two boys began to droop.

'I'm so tired,' Karen said, pointedly looking at their young charges when Nathan stared at her in surprise. 'I think that after pulling, pushing and carrying you two elephants today I know how the reindeer will feel after they've finished pulling the sleigh tonight.'

With cheerful banter and insults going on between them, it wasn't hard to persuade the two boys to take a quiet sleigh ride through the falling snow to their cabin.

The track through the snow-laden trees was marked by lights which looked like small full moons, each of them wearing a halo of swirling snowflakes.

'It's like living inside my little snow thing!' Mark exclaimed. 'A giant must have picked us up and shaken us, and now all the snowflakes are going round and round and landing on everything.'

The two boys were still discussing the possibilities of giants and snowstorms when Karen and Nathan carried them into the cabin and took their outdoor clothing off, but the conversation moved on to a detailed reliving of everything that had happened during the day while they were undressed, washed and put into their pyjamas ready for bed.

'Is there time for Mark and me to have a play with our computer games tonight, Dad?' Matthew asked in a pleading voice that was more asleep than awake.

'Save it for tomorrow, son,' he said quietly into the subdued light of the cabin as he smoothed the back of one finger down the curve of his little-boy cheek. 'There'll be plenty of time to play with computer games, and you never know—if you go to sleep quickly, Father Christmas might even find another little present for you. . .'

He stopped speaking as he realised that both of them were sound asleep and Karen saw him glance across to the little tree in the corner of the cabin.

Suspended from the branches were their presents from Father Christmas—a little group of the small hand-carved ornaments which she had admired when they'd been helping to decorate the big tree earlier.

Matthew's one was the little reindeer with the curving antlers and traditional brightly coloured harness. Mark's was the small replica of Father Christmas himself, complete with red suit and curly white beard. Nathan's memento was the carving of a sleigh with two tiny people in it being taken for a ride, while Karen's was a perfect star which seemed almost to shimmer in the glow of the fire.

In the aftermath of the routine of getting two young boys to bed, the cabin seemed very quiet, but, although

Nathan offered to switch the television on to one of the
English-speaking channels, neither of them was interested in filling the silence with electronic noise.

'Oh!' Karen's preoccupation with the little wooden
ornaments had reminded her of something. 'I've got a
little present for each of the boys and I forgot to give
it to them!' she exclaimed in annoyance, and reached
for the small bag she'd retrieved from its hiding place
and left ready for their return to the cabin that evening.

'I brought them something too, but I was intending
saving it for Christmas Day itself, so they had part of
our English traditions as well.' Nathan reached for the
bag which had served as his camera case throughout
the trip and took out the packages which had been
hidden in the bottom of it.

Karen watched as he crouched down beside the tree
to slide several small packages in brightly coloured
wrapping paper under the lower branches. She went to
take her own small handful of gifts out of the bag which
had been disguising them then paused, remembering
that there was also one in there for Nathan.

When she'd been buying gifts for the two boys at
the airport at Rovaniemi, she'd found herself looking
for something to give him too, but now she was getting
cold feet about it.

What if he hadn't got anything for her? Would that
make him feel awkward, or would he feel more awkward with the idea that she'd bought him anything
at all?

In the end, she did as he had done and slid the parcels
in around the base of the tree. She hadn't actually label-
led the present to him, but she really wanted him to
have it. If he questioned the donor, she could always try
telling him that it had come from Father Christmas. . .

It was still quite early, in spite of the Arctic darkness, and Karen found she couldn't sit still. She had an uncomfortable awareness that she and Nathan were all but marooned together in the small snow-bound cabin.

After a few minutes of unnecessary tidying and putting away around the compact room, Karen reached for her all-in-one suit.

'Are you going somewhere?' Nathan asked in surprise when he saw what she was doing.

'No. Not really,' Karen said, knowing that she had to do something to take her mind off thoughts of him.

He didn't seem in the least bit affected by her proximity and if he should guess what she was feeling. . .

'I—I just wanted to stand out on the porch and watch the snow coming down and listen to the silence. . .' She let her words trail off as she waited for him to say something, half afraid that he would laugh at such foolishness, or, even worse, guess that it was partly a distraction.

'Would you mind if I joined you?' he asked quietly, looking up from his silent contemplation of the fire. 'If we stayed by the door, we'd be able to hear if one of the boys needed us, and it would be lovely to see what the Arctic night feels like—and sounds like—when there are no chattering children to break the silence.'

Karen couldn't help smiling her agreement as warmth spread through her.

He'd understood!

Far from mocking her feelings, Nathan had actually understood what she wanted to do and why she wanted to do it without her having to explain it.

Quietly, they donned their protective clothing and heavy boots and let themselves out of the stout wooden door, Nathan pulling it shut behind them to preserve the heat in the cabin.

Instantly, Karen felt the intense cold, but it was not the bone-chilling feeling of a raw, wet December day in England. *This* was a dry, crisp coldness which almost made the air feel like a chilled sparkling wine.

As they stood at the edge of the overhanging porch, the night seemed to close around them like a strange blanket, the falling snow seeming to deaden all sounds except the wind soughing through the trees which surrounded the cabin.

The thick fresh layer of snow already covering the ground in front of the cabin seemed to glisten in the light escaping from the gap in the curtains at the window.

Momentarily distracted from the scene in front of her, Karen glanced in through the gap at the glimpse she could see of the inside of the cabin.

There was the fire, the logs burning brightly in the midst of the blackened stone surround, and the upturned log stools which had fascinated the boys since they'd first seen them. And there, in the corner, was the little tree with the small pile of parcels underneath, waiting for the morning, and the small carvings swinging gently from its branches in the heat from the fire.

It all looked so warm and cosy—so permanent—but a swift flash of sadness made Karen admit that it was all just an entrancing make-believe. Just like the whole trip, really. . .

'What are you thinking?' Nathan's husky voice was accompanied by puffs of warm breath as he leant towards her. 'You looked so sad for a minute. . .'

Karen drew in a deep breath through the warmth of the wool scarf she'd wrapped over her nose and mouth, debating whether to tell him, then shrugged.

'I was just thinking that nothing is ever quite what it seems,' she admitted eventually.

'In what way?'

'Well, take the cabin, for example.' She gestured with a mittened hand towards the light spilling through the gap in the curtains. 'Anyone looking in there would see the same scene as you'll find on thousands of Christmas cards—the fire burning in the grate, making the room look warm and welcoming, the little tree with the presents underneath, making it look as if a happy family lives there.'

'Is that such a bad thing?' he countered quietly, his dark eyes fixed compellingly on hers. 'Yes, the fire *does* make the room look warm and welcoming, but does that mean it isn't true? And the presents under the tree—they aren't just stage props. The boys will enjoy opening them because they will know that they have been chosen and given with love. The fact that the scene has been set up to look like the picture on a Christmas card won't make any difference to them.'

'I'm sorry,' she murmured, breaking eye contact and looking out into the night. 'It's just. . .' She swung back to face him, her voice urgent. 'He's getting worse, isn't he?'

The words were muffled by the thick woolly scarf but he flinched at their unexpected impact, knowing instantly that she was referring to Mark.

'Yes,' he agreed quietly. 'It looks as if it's suddenly started growing very fast, and it's beginning to invade and cause pressure on vital areas.'

'I noticed that he's started slurring his speech, and he's having difficulties swallowing,' Karen confirmed.

'And he's becoming weaker in his arm and leg on

his left side, too,' Nathan detailed. 'That probably contributed to his fall earlier on today.'

They were silent for a moment and Karen was certain that Nathan's thoughts were travelling the same path as hers were—the realisation that Mark's noticeably worsening condition heralded the imminent end of his young life.

'God! It seems so unfair!' Karen gritted through clenched teeth. 'He's such a lovely little boy and I would do anything I could to help him, but there isn't anything. . .' Her throat closed up and she couldn't continue, the whirling snowflakes blurring as her eyes filled with helpless tears.

'Ah, Karen,' Nathan murmured as he turned her towards him and wrapped his arms comfortingly around her. 'Sometimes I think you're too soft-hearted for your own good.'

'You can't tell me you don't care what's happening to him?' she challenged from the depths of his padded embrace.

'Oh, I care. . .I hate seeing what cancer does to their young lives. I hate what they have to go through, what *I* have to put them through. But, Karen. . .' He paused to fumble one bulky mitten under her chin and tip her head up to face him before he continued, his voice full of concern.

'You're letting it affect you almost as if each one of them was your own child, and it's tearing you apart. You can't afford to do that and nor can I. Eventually it will stop you maintaining the distance you need to help them properly. . .to do your job the way they need it done.'

Karen couldn't meet his eyes without telling the truth.

'You're right, of course.' She sighed dispiritedly.

'But, in fairness, it doesn't happen with every child. Just the little fighters like Mark and Matthew. Somehow they just seem to work their way into your heart. . .' Her emotions got the better of her again and she had to stop.

Nathan was standing very still, his eyes seeming to stare deep inside her as if he wanted to understand what she was thinking, what she was feeling.

'You're a very special woman, Karen March,' he whispered huskily as he cupped the side of her face in one mittened hand. 'I'm so very glad that Matthew and I moved. It was worth all the upheaval just so that he could meet you, could have you caring for him. . .' And he stroked the concealing folds of woollen scarf away from her face to press his cool lips against the warmth of hers.

Karen stiffened in surprise, a startled gasp drawn from her at the unexpectedness of it, and he wrenched his head back as if he was shocked by his own actions.

'I'm. . .I'm sorry, Karen. I didn't mean to. . .' He stumbled to a halt as his eyes travelled over her upturned face.

What he saw there she didn't know, but with a wordless murmur his mouth returned to hers and she folded her arms around him in acceptance.

This was magic, she thought hazily as his lips grew warm against hers. This was what she had been longing for ever since their kiss in the snow. . .no. . .ever since she'd turned round from Matthew's bed and looked for the first time into Nathan's stunning sapphire-blue eyes.

His mouth opened over hers and the tip of his tongue flicked across her lips, painting them in liquid fire until she couldn't bear the torment any more and parted them to allow him access.

A deep groan rumbled from the depths of his chest

and the echoes hovered in the frosty air around their heads, but Karen was oblivious. All she knew was that for the first time in her life she felt as if she was where she belonged.

She'd thought she'd been in love with Gareth until his thoughtless cruelty had made her determined never to let another man into her heart. . .but with Nathan everything was different.

Nathan was different.

She was different.

This time the man in her arms was the one who had taken total possession of her heart; this time she was offering her lips to him, and with them she was offering her whole self, body, heart and mind.

'Nathan,' she breathed when his lips explored the tender skin beneath her jaw, her head pillowed against his broad shoulder when her neck refused to hold its weight any longer. 'Oh, Nathan. . .' And her hand cradled his cheek in turn to direct his lips back to hers.

'God, Karen, what are we doing?' he muttered hoarsely when they both ran out of breath. 'It's minus fifteen out here and it's snowing.'

Karen had tensed when he'd begun to speak, afraid that he was regretting what they'd been doing, but the brief chuckle which followed the words and his tightening grip around her shoulders told her differently.

'I think we're behaving like victims of rampant hormones,' she giggled softly. 'Although I thought it was hot climates that were supposed to have that effect. . .'

'Do you think we'd get away with the impropriety by claiming that we were sharing body heat to keep warm?' He nuzzled his way into the warm hollow where her neck and shoulder met with a husky murmur of pleasure, and she heard him breathe in the scent of her skin.

'Keeping warm,' she croaked as her knees turned to silly putty. 'You could provide the power for a fair-sized town on the heat we're generating. . .' Her laughter disappeared under his mouth as he renewed his assault on her senses.

It wasn't until she felt him fumbling to find the fastenings for her all-in-one suit that she began to draw away from him.

'Nathan. . .we can't,' she said, capturing his hands and holding them still.

A brief huff of white steam drifting away from his head confirmed the exasperated sound she heard.

'I know, Karen. I know. We can't do anything more than kiss because it's below freezing out here and there are two little boys in there. . .but that doesn't mean that I don't want to, because I do.'

His eyes were almost fierce in the strange light and Karen felt a quiver deep inside her when she recognised the sincerity in his tone.

'I know,' she whispered softly, and squeezed his captive hands.

'And you do too,' he said boldly, the words a statement rather than a question.

'Did I leave you in any doubt?' She couldn't believe that the brazen words were hers and felt the heat climb her cheeks in spite of the cold surrounding them.

'If only there was some way we could—'

'No,' she interrupted. 'It's probably better this way. We've got those two in there depending on us.'

'You're right, of course. Eminently sensible.' He gave a rueful chuckle. 'And to think that just a few minutes ago I was accusing you of being too emotional!'

He bent to place a tender kiss on her sensitive lips. 'One last kiss to tide me over until we find a more suitable time and place,' he grumbled, and turned to open the door for her.

After they'd shed their outerwear, Karen left Nathan checking up on the two boys and stoking the fire while she took first turn in the little bathroom.

For several minutes she just gazed at herself in the mirror, her cheeks bright and her dark brown eyes shining. With the tip of one wondering finger she traced the new fullness of her lips and felt the sharp twist of arousal deep inside her body.

'Nathan,' she whispered softly, then gave her head a disgusted shake. Anyone would think that she was an adolescent mooning over the latest heartthrob—and there was no doubt that Nathan could make *her* heart throb, and thunder and gallop. . .

'Get under that shower, you silly woman,' she muttered crossly. 'Any more nonsense and it had better be a cold one. . .' She shuddered at the thought of it and reached for the soap.

'Can we open the presents now?' Matthew demanded, his voice shrill with excitement as he bounced up and down on the edge of the double bunk while Karen struggled to finish putting his boots on.

The two lads didn't notice the small collection of parcels which had appeared under the tree since they'd gone to bed until the sleigh which would take them across to the main cabin was announcing its arrival outside their cabin with the jingle of bells.

It took some rapid, world-class diplomacy on Nathan's part to persuade the two of them to postpone the delights of parcel-opening until they returned to the cabin after breakfast, but the promise of seeing ice lanterns and log torches finally won the day.

The simple Christmas service was held in the open air, lit only by guttering flames, and the mixture of voices rising into the early morning Arctic darkness as they sang inside the circle of light was something Karen thought she'd never forget.

Mark and Matthew were well wrapped against the cold in the shelter of the sleigh and the service became even more magical for Karen when Nathan came to stand behind her and wrapped an arm around her waist to pull her back into the shelter of his bigger, broader body.

She was almost disappointed when the echoes of the last hymn were lost among the tree-clad slopes because it would mean the end of this seductive closeness.

A deep rumble broke into her thoughts.

'What was that?' She looked around for the source of the noise but couldn't see anything.

'Well,' Nathan began with a twinkle in his eye and a wink for the two boys, 'either it was a warning of an earthquake or the reindeer was having a grumble about having to drag these two elephants around or. . .'

'Or what?' the boys demanded with grins for his nonsense.

'Or it was my stomach rumbling because I'm starving!' he finished, with a comical look of agony on his face. 'Let's go and eat!'

CHAPTER NINE

BREAKFAST was a hearty affair full of jokes and good
humour, but all the time there was an underlying tension
between Karen and Nathan over Mark's gradual deterioration, their eyes meeting across the table as she lent
the boy a helping hand.

'Do you think we should find out if it's possible to
go back to England today?' Karen asked in a hastily
muttered aside after the meal was over.

Mark had been having trouble, now that his left side
was becoming paralysed, but she hoped she'd managed
to make her help surreptitious enough to save him the
embarrassment of making a mess in public.

Her main worry was the deeper significance of the
events.

'I'll make enquiries about the availability of alternative flights,' Nathan agreed. 'But I'd rather keep to the
proper itinerary if at all possible—he's only going to
get one shot at this trip and I don't want to drag him
home if there's any way of letting him stay.'

'Right.' Karen smiled over her fears, knowing she
could trust his judgement. 'I know he's having a particularly bad patch at the moment and the symptoms could
stay at this level for some time before they worsen.'
When she looked up at Nathan, she allowed all her
concern to show. 'I'm just worried for his parents' sake,
in case anything happens when he's so far away from
them. . .'

'Obviously there are no guarantees,' he said softly

as he moved aside for their waitress, Maritta Aho, to approach the table. For a moment he smiled as he paused to watch the cheerful young woman talking to the boys. As usual, she began by greeting them in Lappish then coached their replies in the same language.

The smile faded when he turned back to continue their conversation, and became the more serious expression Karen was accustomed to seeing when they worked together at the hospital.

'Look, Karen, we're both here keeping an eye on him and I promise that at the first sign that things are beginning to get out of hand I'll arrange for him to fly back to England—even if it means I have to accompany him back myself and leave you here with Matthew to follow on later.'

As there was nothing more to be said, they turned back to the table to find out why the two boys seemed so excited.

'Maritta told us about the skidoos,' Matthew announced importantly, obviously acting as spokesman for the two of them. 'She says we can learn how to drive one if we have a grown-up on the back with us.'

'Can we do it?' Mark pleaded. 'Can we drive one?'

Karen and Nathan exchanged glances as they weighed up the possible problems, then he gave a surreptitious nod.

'I don't know,' Nathan said with an exaggerated frown. 'What do you think, Karen?'

'They'd have to promise not to go too fast,' Karen said just as seriously. 'I'd get frightened if they went so fast that we took off like an aeroplane.'

'You're teasing us!' Matthew exclaimed indignantly.

'A skidoo can't go fast enough to take off—can it, Maritta?'

She laughed and shook her head.

'In that case, I don't see any reason why we can't have a go at it,' Nathan decided with an infectious grin. 'Let's grab our outdoor clothes and go!'

The controls on the machines were very simple to operate and in no time Nathan and Mark were paired on one, with Karen and Matthew on the other, as they set off along a track leading away from the complex and into the surrounding forest.

Karen sat behind Matthew, her arms surrounding him as she rested her hands on the handlebars beside his little mittened paws until he got the hang of it.

'Noisy, isn't it?' she called back to Nathan as he followed behind with Mark, the silence of the woods shattered by a sound which rivalled a cross between a moped and a lawnmower.

They followed the marked trail through the snow-laden trees for some way into the woods before they switched off the engines and allowed the silence to return.

'It feels as if we're the only people left in the world,' Matthew whispered. 'There are no people and no houses.'

'But it doesn't feel lonely, does it?' Karen commented, feeling as if she too ought to keep her voice down—almost as if she was in a church. 'You feel as if you could go just round the corner and find a nomads' camp or a complete village if you wanted to.'

All four sat in silence for several minutes as they looked around at the amazing variety of trees under the covering of snow. Some were the traditional conical shape of Christmas trees, while others towered high in the air like the soaring pillars in some lofty cathedral.

'Are you ready to go back?' Nathan finally said as he looked across at Karen.

Although they were growing tired, the boys initially said they wanted to go on exploring further—until Karen reminded them that they still had some presents to open. Then they could hardly get back to the cabin fast enough.

'Right, now,' Nathan began as soon as they were settled in the cosy warmth of the cabin. 'What have we here?' He reached for the nearest package and read the label. 'It says Mark.' He carried it over and Karen helped to steady it while the youngster ripped the paper away in handfuls.

'It's another game for the computer,' he crowed in delight. 'Great! I haven't tried this one before.'

'And now one for Matthew,' Nathan announced as he delivered it.

'I've got a game too!' he shouted excitedly. 'It's a different one to yours, Mark, so we'll be able to swop.'

'And now another one each. A soft one,' Nathan said quickly, before the two of them got totally wrapped up in their computers.

'It's a. . .it's a T-shirt,' Matthew said as he held it up.

'So's mine. And it's got Father Christmas on it. Look!' He spread it out across his knees to display the picture of a very familiar gentleman and his reindeer-drawn sleigh.

'There's some writing on it too,' Karen pointed out. 'Can you read what it says?'

' "I met Father Christmas in Lapland," ' Mark deciphered with a little bit of prompting from Nathan.

Forestalling the possibility that the boys would immediately strip off to try the T-shirts on, Karen suggested that they should wear them to return to England to show Mark's parents.

'That just leaves these two,' Nathan said as he reached for the last packages under the tree. 'Strange. They're the same shape and the same size, but only one of them has a name on it.' He handed one of them to Karen who immediately recognised his writing from the number of times she saw it in the course of a day at the hospital.

They tore away the wrappings simultaneously and both began to laugh.

'Snap!' Nathan said as he turned the small framed picture towards Karen who raised an identical one to face him.

'What is it?' Matthew demanded. 'What did you get?'

'They're pictures of Lapland in the autumn,' Karen explained, turning the picture towards him. 'It's called *ruska*, and when they get the right combination of night frosts and rain everything looks as if it's been painted red, yellow and gold, just like the picture.'

'But why were you laughing? And why have you got two of them?'

'Because Karen and I both chose the same thing for each other without knowing,' Nathan said with a smile, his eyes meeting hers across the room.

'They're not as good as our computer games,' Matthew declared stoutly. 'Can we play with them now?'

Nathan glanced at his watch.

'That depends on whether you want to have your lunch in an igloo.'

'An igloo?' Their imagination was caught and it took

very little effort to encourage them to get ready for the new experience.

Once again, they were sitting on upturned log seats while they ate, but it was obvious that the igloo itself was the main attraction for the boys.

'I thought it would be cold, like sitting in a fridge,' Matthew confided in a stage whisper after a few minutes. 'Why is it all warm in here?'

'And why doesn't the snow melt?' Mark demanded.

'An igloo is made out of a special sort of snow—a very hard snow that we can cut into blocks for building,' one of the staff explained. 'We can only build igloos when there is this snow here.'

'And why is it warm in here?' Matthew repeated, intrigued by the details.

'Because the walls are so thick that they don't let the warm from the fire get out or the cold from outside get in—just enough cold gets through the walls to stop them from melting.'

By the time they'd finished eating, both boys were ready for a rest and didn't put up any more than a token argument before they settled down on their bunks for a short nap.

'Apparently it's traditional to have a sauna on Christmas Day before the evening meal,' Nathan murmured softly as he stretched his long legs out towards the crackling log fire. 'Do you want to try it?'

'I—I don't know,' Karen stammered, her heart suddenly racing inside her chest. What was Nathan suggesting—that they share a sauna?

'Personally,' he continued, with a heated glance over her slim-fitting jeans and cream-coloured mohair sweater, 'I think the Finns are spoilsports because they insist that a sauna is strictly for bathing and meditating, relaxing and talking and even for giving birth, but never for making babies.'

Karen felt the heat engulf her face at the thought that he might have been reading her mind.

If she was naked in a sauna with Nathan Beckett, she was quite certain that the last thing she would be doing was relaxing. . .

'I could get it ready and then we could take turns if you like,' he offered, his words cutting across her lascivious thoughts.

'Well. . .OK,' she capitulated, knowing it was what she wanted to do anyway. 'I can hardly come to Finland and stay in a cabin with its own sauna without trying it once.'

The hotel had thoughtfully provided instructions for their foreign visitors who might not be familiar with Finnish saunas and Karen emerged half an hour later feeling as if she was glowing all over.

'You look about sixteen,' a husky voice growled from behind her, and she turned to find Nathan's eyes raking her scrubbed and shining face and her hair, darkened by water and plastered to her head.

'Y-your turn,' she stammered as she stepped out of his way, wrapping her arms around herself and hugging her dressing-gown to her almost defensively. 'There are lots of towels. . .' And she fled ignominiously, suddenly afraid that if he did reach out a hand to touch her as his eyes were telling her he wanted to she wouldn't be able to stop him because it was what she wanted too.

The boys woke soon after and, when they'd had a drink, were perfectly happy to compete against each other on their computer games until it was time to go across for dinner.

'You will be coming to the dance this evening?' Maritta asked as she served their meals.

'No.' Karen smiled as she tamped down the wistful thoughts. 'We'll be going back to the cabin with the boys.'

'Ah, but this is not right!' the young woman exclaimed. 'You must come dancing for Christmas. I will come to your cabin to sit with your boys.'

'That's very kind of you,' Nathan began. 'But I don't think that. . .'

'I have two brothers,' she volunteered quickly. 'I look after them when I am at home. And when I finish school I will be doing nursing.' She glanced meaningfully at Mark and Karen realised that she was trying to let them know as tactfully as possible that she understood their worries. 'I can use the telephone in the cabin to call you if the boys need you,' she added persuasively.

'What do you think, Karen?' Nathan challenged. 'Are you brave enough to let me tread on your toes?'

Before she could answer, Matthew butted in.

'Are you any good at computer games?' he demanded, his eyes fixed firmly on Maritta. 'Mark and me got some games from Father Christmas.'

'I can beat both my brothers on theirs,' Maritta replied with a smile. 'What games have you got?'

'It looks as if our evening has been arranged for us,' Nathan commented wryly as the three of them began talking about their scores on various different games. 'Unless you'd rather not?'

Karen felt the smile curving her lips and had to bite the tip of her tongue between her teeth to prevent herself laughing out loud.

'I think it would be lovely,' she said, amazed at how

calm she sounded when every nerve in her body was pulsing with electricity. She was going to be dancing with Nathan tonight; he was going to hold her in his arms and they were going to move around the room while the music played in the background. . .

'What time do you want me to come to your cabin?' Maritta asked, jolting Karen back to her senses. 'The dance will start at nine.'

Karen was still in the bathroom when she heard Nathan call out that he was going to collect Maritta from the main cabin, and she had to chuckle. He sounded just like a long-suffering husband accustomed to a wife who was never ready on time.

The smile faded.

Perhaps he sounded that way because his wife *had* always kept him waiting. How was she to know? She'd hardly known him long enough for them to exchange many confidences; in fact she hardly knew any more than the basic details about him.

The one thing she *did* know without any doubt was that she was completely and irrevocably in love with him.

Oh, she'd known she admired him long before they'd set off for this trip, both as a man and as a doctor. But it was his wonderful gentleness and patience with the two boys, and his unselfconscious ability to put himself in their place and know how to talk to them and play with them, which had finally tipped the balance.

'Are you ready yet?' Matthew's voice called, and she suddenly realised that she was still standing there with her lipstick in her hand. 'Dad will be back in a minute and you said we could see you in your dress-up clothes.'

Karen laughed softly as she rapidly scooped everything into her wash kit and left the bathroom. 'Talk about like father, like son,' she said to herself.

'Well? What do you think?' She twirled round to let the boys see the fine, silky fabric of her wide-legged evening trousers flare out then subside, to cling to her slender legs like a slim skirt.

'I like the goldy bits,' Mark murmured as he reached out to trace the bugle beads which made up the pattern of autumn leaves across the draped bodice of the matching top.

'Thank you, kind sirs.' Karen dropped them a curtsey. 'Now I'd better get my outdoor clothes on so I'm ready when he comes back with Maritta.'

Karen wasn't certain, but she thought she saw disappointment cross Nathan's face when he arrived at the cabin with their baby-sitter and found that she'd already hidden her outfit under her all-in-one suit.

'She's got trousers on, Dad,' Matthew told him, his eyes obviously missing nothing when his father asked if Karen was ready.

'And goldy bits,' Mark added cryptically before his attention returned to his computer game.

They'd been walking along the snowy path towards the main cabin for several minutes before Nathan broke the silence.

'I'm sorry I didn't think of it before, but I should have asked if you really wanted to go to the dance. We were rather bulldozed into it by the youngsters and, well, I know you women like to be properly dressed for an occasion. It just didn't occur to me that you might have to wear trousers and feel out of place—'

'Nathan.' Karen interrupted his rambling apology, glad that her scarf was hiding her mischievous smile.

'You don't have to worry. I'm quite happy to wear my trousers tonight. Honestly.'

'Trousers and goldy bits,' he muttered with a wry grin when she finally shed her padding in the warmth of the main cabin. 'I can see I'm going to have to instruct my son on the finer points of stunning evening wear.'

He took her elbow to lead her through towards the music, pausing briefly to glance over her from the shining bell of her freshly washed hair to the slender, strappy-heeled sandals she'd carried across from the cabin to change into.

'Stunning,' he repeated huskily, his eyes darkening with appreciation. 'Absolutely stunning. . .' And he led her through to the dance-floor.

The music flowed over them as Nathan guided her around the floor, one hand positioned correctly on her back, the other wrapped around hers to hold it against his chest.

In honour of the special occasion, the room was completely lit by candles, the soft golden glow highlighting the bright gleams in Nathan's hair and making his eyes shine deeply blue as he gazed down at her.

It wasn't long before Karen's desire to be held closer was answered as he closed the distance between them and wrapped both arms around her, drawing her head down to rest against his shoulder.

'Karen,' he whispered against her temple, almost as if he enjoyed the sound of her name, the soft puff of his breath stirring her silky hair against her cheek.

'Mmm?' She turned her head to look up at him and accidentally brushed her lips against the corner of his mouth—or was it an accident?

Deep inside, the contact caused a sharp twist of

awareness, and when he drew in a shuddering breath she knew that he was just as affected by it as she was.

'Don't,' he groaned as she gazed up at him. 'Don't look at me like that or I'm going to scandalise everyone.'

'H-how?' She swallowed convulsively, as if that would stop her pulse beating furiously at the base of her throat.

'I'll probably do something totally insane like throw you over my shoulder and race out into the darkness.'

Karen giggled at the mental image of the dignified consultant oncologist tipping her over his shoulder and running out into the night, then remembered the temperature outside and shuddered.

'You'd better not,' she warned. 'We'd freeze to death out there.'

He muttered something under his breath but when she caught sight of the disgruntled expression on his face she didn't dare ask what he'd said.

They danced for nearly an hour, outwardly relaxed and happy to be there, but Karen could feel the tension building between them in spite of her efforts at innocuous conversation.

Gradually, his monosyllabic answers sapped her enthusiasm and she couldn't help being aware of the set expression which had taken over his face.

'Dammit!' Nathan muttered explosively when the tempo became even slower, and he released his hold on her to take her by the hand. 'I've had enough of this. We're going back to the cabin,' he declared, and virtually dragged her off the floor and out to collect their clothing.

Karen felt sick.

Their romantic evening was spoilt and she didn't even know why.

A swift glance at Nathan's face as they left the main cabin to make their way back convinced her that it wasn't worth asking him—he looked so angry. . .

'Thank you so much for staying with the boys,' Karen said to Maritta a few minutes later with a stiff smile pinned to her face. 'We had a lovely evening. . .' She closed the door as Nathan escorted Maritta down the cabin steps and then fled across the dimly lit cabin.

She got as far as the door to the little bathroom before the tears started to fall, and she quickly shut herself inside. She didn't want her crying to wake the boys or she'd have to try to explain why. . .and she didn't *know* why.

'Karen?'

It was Nathan's voice. He was outside the door and she hadn't even heard him return from walking Maritta back. She smoothed her fingers across her cheeks to try to remove the tracks the tears had made.

'Karen? Are you all right?' The words were accompanied by a gentle tapping on the door.

'Just a minute.' She ran the cold tap over her fingers and pressed them to her eyes in a vain attempt at cooling the heat, but she was never going to be able to totally hide the fact that she'd been crying ever since he left.

She reached out one hand towards the door, drew in a slow, deep breath and released it before she pulled the door open.

'I'm sorry to keep you waiting,' she murmured, tilting her head forward so that her hair would hide as much of her face as possible. 'You can have the bathroom now.'

She went to walk past him but he caught her elbow and swung her round to face him.

'What's the matter, Karen? Aren't you feeling well?' He tilted her face up towards his with a gentle hand. 'What's happened. . .? You've been crying!' It was almost an accusation. 'Why?'

'Shh! You'll disturb the boys,' she reminded him as she turned her face away in embarrassment.

'Dammit!' he muttered, and pushed open the door of the sauna with one hand and pulled her in after him. 'Now, tell me what's going on.'

She'd had every intention of being strong but it was the concern in his eyes which started the tears falling again.

'Oh, Karen. I'm sorry.' He pulled her into his arms and cradled her gently, rocking her as if she were a child who needed comfort.

He held her in silence for a long time before he started to speak in a husky murmur.

'I'm sorry to have been so. . .rough this evening,' he began, the words slightly uneven and gravelly, as though it was hard for him to say them. 'It's been such a long time since I've been attracted to a woman— since I've even *noticed* a woman—that I must have just assumed. . .'

'Assumed?' Karen repeated, completely puzzled.

'That you felt the same way as I do,' he murmured, his voice deeper than ever. 'That you wanted me as much as I want you. . .'

'You. . .' Suddenly Karen was as short of breath as if she'd been winded. To go from agony to near ecstasy in the space of a heartbeat. . .'You want me?' she repeated in disbelief.

'God, yes, I want you,' he said fiercely. 'What do you think that was all about? If I'd stayed there with you in my arms for one more dance I'd have thrown you down on the dance-floor and damn the consequences!'

Karen swallowed to try to hold down the bubbles of happiness which were trying to float her right off her feet.

'If we'd danced one more dance,' she said in a shaky voice, 'it would have taken the toss of a coin to decide who was going to be thrown on the floor first!'

There were several seconds of silence while Karen felt the scalding heat crawl up her throat and into her face, wondering if her sudden boldness had shocked him, before a deep rumble of laughter filled the small wood-panelled room.

'Oh, thank God,' he said in a heartfelt groan as he held her tightly and searched for her mouth with his.

'The Finns would definitely *not* approve of this,' Karen murmured as she lay draped bonelessly over Nathan's broad, naked chest in the aftermath of their explosive desire.

Nathan chuckled, the sensation travelling right through her body and rekindling the aftershocks which had just begun to die away.

'I won't tell them if you don't,' he promised as he lifted his head from the slatted wooden bench they'd ended up on to press a kiss to her love-swollen lips. 'Anyway, we weren't having a sauna—just taking advantage of the residual warmth in here and the fact that it's the only place where I could have my wicked way with you without the possibility of onlookers.'

'Oh, Lord! The children!' she moaned guiltily. 'I didn't give them another thought.'

'I'm pleased to hear it.' He stroked both hands down her back and cupped the smooth curves of her bottom, tilting his hips to remind her that they were still intimately joined. 'I don't think my ego could have taken the competition.'

He fell silent and Karen luxuriated in the pleasure of lying so close to him that she couldn't tell where he ended and she began.

He was everything she'd imagined—tall, strong and handsome, but also gentle, considerate and passionate. . .

'Why?' he murmured into her hair, the word hardly more than a breath of air.

'Hmm?' Had she missed something, drifting in her own dream world?

'Why me? Why now?' he demanded quietly, and she froze.

'Wh-what do you mean?' she quavered, hoping he didn't mean what she feared. She'd honestly believed that he hadn't noticed that brief moment of tension when the pain had struck her so unexpectedly.

'Come on, Karen! I've just made love to you—what do you think I mean?' he said, his voice showing his exasperation. 'You're a virgin, so why. . .?'

'I *was* a virgin,' she pointed out softly as she lifted her head from the comfort of his shoulder, defying her cheeks to redden. 'And as to why, you only have to look in the mirror.'

'So I was just some sort of convenience?' His husky tones were roughened by some unknown emotion. 'You only wanted me for my body?'

'No!' She reached up and swiftly covered his mouth with kisses. 'No. You're not just a body, you're. . . you're the only person who has ever set me on fire.'

She bit her lip, half regretting the admission until he groaned and speared his fingers through her hair to bring her mouth down to his again.

'Dammit!' he muttered. 'How can I do this properly when I daren't move in case I tip you on the floor?'

'Well, then. You've got a choice,' she suggested with a mischievous grin. 'You can either do it improperly, or else start off on the floor so we can't fall.'

'Or do it improperly on the floor,' he growled as he swiped at the remaining pile of thick, fluffy towels so that they landed on the pine-panelled floor. 'Now,' he said as he laid her back on the makeshift bed and combed his fingers through the damp silk of her hair. 'Now I can show you what it's all about. . .' And he lowered his body over hers until they became one.

Their last day in Lapland was filled with all the boys' favourite activities and Nathan must have filled several films with the photos he took.

He took shots of each of them supported safely while they tried to ride a reindeer and their first attempts at driving one of the mini-skidoos all by themselves.

Karen was given a crash-course in photography when Nathan devised a way of taking each of the boys down a gentle slope on the front of his skis so that they could experience at first hand the thrill of the air rushing past their faces at speed.

'It's like flying!' Mark enthused when he'd had his third turn. 'I feel as if I could take off and go up into the sky!'

But it was their final trip which affected Karen the most—a trip through the silence of the twilit forest to an isolated hilltop later that afternoon, when the sky cleared and the stars emerged to glitter like diamonds scattered on inky velvet.

'Is that where heaven is?' Matthew said into the silence, his head tilted back against his father's shoulder as he gazed up at stars that seemed so much bigger and brighter and closer than they'd ever looked in England.

'I don't know,' Nathan admitted huskily, and Karen's heart went out to him. He loved his son so much, and the thought that he might not win the fight against the leukaemia which was trying to claim him was eating the poor man away from the inside.

'My grandmother had a theory,' she offered. 'She thought that every star was once a person and when they died they became stars so that they could still see the people they'd left behind and let them know they loved them.'

'Will I be a star?' Mark asked quietly. 'I would like to be able to look down and see people looking up at me.'

'I think you can be anything you want to be,' Karen murmured as she surreptitiously wiped away a tear.

'Then nobody would be able to forget me,' he whispered, almost as if he was talking to himself, and the thought seemed to ease a strange tension in him.

CHAPTER TEN

THEY'D only been back at the hospital five days when Mark's parents were ready to be released. Both were still wearing casts but between them, and with help from caring neighbours, they would manage.

Besides, Mark needed to go home.

The deterioration which had started while he was in Lapland had seemed to accelerate once they were back in England, and Karen knew he was going home to die.

'We can't thank you enough for what you and Mr Beckett did for Mark,' the Hoopers said when they came up to the ward to collect him. 'He's gone over those photos every time he's visited us and told us everything that happened—especially about talking to Father Christmas.'

'He was a very special man,' Karen confirmed, remembering the tears she'd seen in the old gentleman's eyes when he'd made his farewells to Mark and Matthew on Christmas Eve.

'Well, he certainly made an impression on the two boys,' Mrs Hooper said. 'Neither one of them will let those little carvings out of their sight.'

Karen smiled. Mrs Hooper was right. Mark might have completely lost the use of his left hand now, but his little carving of Father Christmas was usually clutched tightly in his right hand, and if he was busy with his computer games it was always propped up where he could see it easily.

Matthew, too, seemed to regard his little reindeer as

some sort of magic mascot, in spite of the fact that he still hadn't been well enough to go home yet. He'd been holding it tightly just this morning when they'd done the latest set of tests to see how well he'd responded to his treatment.

The whole ward turned out to wave Mark goodbye.

The younger patients just thought he was going home, but the older ones, and their parents, realised what was really happening and the staff knew from experience that there was the possibility that over the next few days some of them might show adverse reactions to the event, relating it to their own situation.

That evening, one of the other patients with acute lymphoblastic leukaemia was very tearful, but it was Matthew who was the worst hit and it happened very suddenly.

Oh, Karen knew that he and Mark had been inseparable since they'd first met, but Matthew had always been such a positive little character, such a fighter, that Karen wasn't really prepared for the black gloom which suddenly descended over him, and which nothing seemed to penetrate.

'Karen.'

Nathan's husky voice made her lift her head from her contemplation of the pile of paperwork she'd been ploughing her way through to see him standing in the doorway, his hands buried in the pockets of his dark grey suit.

A swift pang pierced her like an arrow when she saw how tired he looked.

He'd hardly spoken to her since they'd returned from the trip, unless there was someone else in the room. He couldn't have made it any clearer that he regretted what had happened between them without hanging a banner across the front of the hospital.

She smiled wryly at the joyous memory that thought evoked of the wonderful send-off the ward had arranged for Mark and Matthew when they'd left for Lapland.

'Take a seat.' Karen waved him into the comfortable chair he'd made his own in happier times as she left her own to go across to the tray in the corner. 'Coffee?'

He accepted half-heartedly and barely remembered his manners when she handed him the steaming mug.

'What can I do for you?' she prompted when the silence seemed to go on for ever. 'A problem with one of the patients?'

'It's Matthew.' He sighed, finally raising his eyes to meet hers, and she could have wept at the pain that filled them. 'Since Mark went home I can't get through to him and he won't tell me what's wrong.' He spoke reluctantly, his voice rough as though it hurt to say the words.

'How can I help?' she offered, knowing that she'd be willing to do anything he asked; anything to bring back the brightness to his beautiful dark blue eyes.

'Will you talk to him?' he asked hesitantly, as though hating to have to ask for her help. 'Can you see if he'll tell you what's going on inside his head?'

'Have you told him about the latest test results? Does he know that they weren't good?'

'I haven't dared—not without knowing what's made him so depressed.'

'He'll have to know soon,' she warned. 'He's been through the system long enough to know when you start doing something different, and he'll ask why.'

'He will, won't he?' There was a wry pride in the words at the thought that a six-year-old could keep him on his toes.

'When do you want me to have a go? After you've gone home this evening? Or would you rather be somewhere near at hand, in case he needs to speak to you afterwards?'

He speared his fingers restlessly through his hair, leaving the smooth dark blond strands uncharacteristically tousled.

'I'd rather it wasn't necessary at all,' he muttered. 'I don't know why he's cut himself off from me like this. We've been fighting this together all along and now suddenly. . .'

'Right,' Karen said decisively. 'I'll wait until the ward quietens down a little this evening. If there's the sound of television going on it'll mask the sound of voices so he won't be worried about being overheard.'

'But. . .'

Karen could see how much it would frustrate him not to know what was happening so she quickly suggested an alternative.

'If you sit yourself in here where he can't see you, you'll be able to watch for my signal if I need to call you over.'

'*If* you need to,' he repeated pessimistically. 'I don't mind telling you I'm at my wits' end.'

'And it makes it worse because you love him,' Karen said softly, knowing just how deep the bond between them was.

'I'd do anything for him,' he vowed fiercely. 'Anything!'

*   *   *

By the time Karen finally approached Matthew's bed, it was much later than she'd intended and she wasn't certain whether he was still awake.

There had been a major catastrophe not far from the hospital with a block of flats devastated by a gas explosion and every ward had been asked to shuffle patients to make more room for the injured.

She and Nathan had been forced to delay putting their plan into action until he was free from the sudden rush of paediatric emergencies.

In the event, it had been easy for him to position himself out of sight in Sister's office because Matthew was curled up on his side facing away from the viewing window, and had been for several hours.

'Matthew?' Karen said softly. If he was asleep, she wouldn't wake him, much as she longed to find out what was making him so miserable.

'Yes?' The sad little voice emerged from the curled-up figure.

'Can I come and keep you company for a little while? I've got no one else to talk to.'

She waited silently, knowing that it had to be *his* decision.

'OK.' He sighed.

Karen positioned a chair beside his bed and sat down. She'd thought about sitting on the side of the bed to get close to him but decided that even at six years old he had the right to decide whether to make contact with her.

This way, if he wanted to reach out to her, she was close enough, and if he didn't she wasn't forcing herself on him.

The silence between them went on for nearly five

minutes, and Karen was just beginning to despair when he uncurled slightly and glanced across at her.

'Mark's gone home to die,' he said in a wobbly voice, and Karen bit her lip at the sadness in his little face.

'I know,' she murmured evenly, knowing that this sort of heartbreaking conversation would happen again and again all the while she was nursing such sick children. The only thing she could do was take it at *his* pace.

So she waited. And waited.

'If my tests are bad, I'm going to die too.' The words emerged flatly and she saw the soft yellow light strike the tell-tale shiny streak on his cheek which marked the track of a tear.

For a moment she contemplated trying to give him false hope, just so that he would have something to hold onto, but it wouldn't have been fair. He had spent so much time in his young life around children who were stricken with terminal illnesses that he was coming to terms with the concept of death on a personal level long before he should have.

'If your tests are bad, that just means that the course of chemotherapy didn't do what we wanted it to, but your dad will try something else to get you better. He's already put you on the computer for a bone marrow transplant.' She took a chance and touched his hand. 'He won't be giving up, even if the tests *are* bad.'

She was heartened when he didn't pull his hand away from the contact with hers, but there was another long silence while he wrestled with his thoughts.

'But what about when I die? He'll give up then,' he said sadly, and looked down at his clenched hand, uncurling the little fingers just far enough for her to see the curving antlers and brightly painted harness of the little wooden reindeer.

Karen wasn't quite sure what he meant, but she didn't dare interrupt to ask because she had a feeling that they were finally getting to his biggest fear and she didn't want him to stop speaking—not before he'd told her what it was.

'Father Christmas said that when I looked at Rudolph I should remember that wishes can come true—but they haven't!' The disillusionment in his voice was very different from the enthralment of the child who'd spoken trustingly to the man in the familiar red suit.

'What did you wish that hasn't come true?' she prompted softly. 'Perhaps it's a wish that needs a bit of help—like Mark's wish to go to see Father Christmas.'

'The Wish people can't do it. Only Daddy.' There was such iron-clad certainty in his voice.

'Have you asked him?'

He shook his head wordlessly.

'Is it very important?'

'Yes,' he whispered. 'Very important.'

'Then don't you think you ought to ask him, just in case he *can* do it?' she urged. 'I know he loves you very much and I'm sure he'd do it if he could.'

There was another long silence while Karen secretly crossed her fingers under the edge of the bedclothes.

At one point, Matthew pulled his hand away from hers and her heart sank when she thought that she'd failed, but as she watched he opened his clenched fist to gaze thoughtfully at the little reindeer.

'OK,' he said, his voice more positive than she'd heard it for some time. 'I'll ask him.'

Karen sent up a silent prayer of thanks that she'd apparently managed to handle the situation correctly.

'Do you want me to find him and send him to you?'

she offered, worried that he might change his mind if he had too much time to think about it.

'Will you bring him?' He suddenly fixed her with an intense gaze before looking back down at the reindeer and squeezing it tightly in his hand. 'I need you to bring him with you,' he insisted.

Karen promised to bring him as soon as possible and hurried across to Sister's office.

'Well?' Nathan demanded anxiously as soon as she came through the door. She was certain that only the possibility that Matthew might see him had kept him glued to his chair although now he was leaning forward eagerly with his hands clenched into fists on his knees. 'Did he tell you anything?'

'Yes and no. . .' She held her hand up to halt the threatened explosion.

'He's a six-year-old struggling with the concept of death in relation to himself and those around him. *He* told *me* that Mark had gone home to die. . .'

Nathan began to look grey, as though he could guess what was coming next.

'Then he told me that if the results on that last lot of tests were bad he was going to die too.'

'Dammit! Does he think that I'm just going to give up on him?' Nathan's low voice was anguished. 'He must know that I'd do anything possible. . .'

'That's what I told him,' Karen stressed. 'I reminded him that his name was on the computer for a bone marrow transplant.'

'And?'

'He said that Father Christmas was wrong—that wishes don't come true.'

'What has he been wishing for? The tests to come back perfect?'

'No. He said it was a wish that only you could make come true.'

'Then why wouldn't he *tell* me? He can have whatever he wants. . .'

'I think he was expecting his little reindeer to perform some magic, until I reminded him that sometimes wishes need people like Make-A-Wish to help them come true.'

'Did that help?'

'Yes.' Karen nodded. 'He says he's going to ask you, but for some reason I've got to be there too. . .'

Karen didn't know why, but her stomach was full of butterflies as she followed Nathan through the muted sounds and shadows of the ward to his son's bedside. She had the strangest feeling that something momentous was going to happen once they joined Matthew in his little circle of light.

'Hello, Matthew,' Nathan said softly as he sat himself down in the chair Karen had so recently vacated.

'Dad.' Matthew rolled onto his back and scooted himself up against the slope of the white pillows.

'Karen tells me you've got another wish,' he began tentatively. 'Something you want me to do?'

Matthew nodded, the light shining down on the emerging regrowth which, God willing, would one day grow back as thick and strong as his father's dark blond hair.

For several seconds they all watched his small hands fondling the little reindeer before he fixed his deep blue gaze directly on his father's face and said clearly, 'I want you to get married.'

'What?' Nathan sounded as shocked as Karen felt. 'Why?' He was gazing intently at his son as if he wanted to see the thoughts which had produced this preposterous idea. 'Why do you want me to get *married*?'

For a second, Matthew looked fearful and his eyes dropped to the little reindeer again. Then, as if he'd drawn new courage from it, Karen saw him square his little shoulders and tilt his chin up to face his father.

'Because when I die I don't want you to be lonely. I don't want you to be all by yourself,' he said firmly.

'But. . .' Nathan was speechless.

'Karen said you would do it,' he said insistently. 'She said you could make it happen.'

There was a roaring sound in Karen's ears as she heard her words being quoted so desperately. What on earth was Nathan thinking? She'd had no idea that *this* was what Matthew wanted. If she'd known, she would at least have asked him if he'd chosen a candidate. . .

'Who do you want me to marry?' Nathan's husky words were the ones she hadn't had the chance to say herself. What if she had to watch the man she loved get married to another woman. . .?

'Karen, of course,' Matthew said as though exasperated with his father's slow comprehension.

Suddenly, as Nathan turned towards her and their eyes met, the air became too heavy to breathe and she shook her head wordlessly, unable to tell him that she hadn't known what Matthew was going to say.

'Perhaps she doesn't want to, son,' he suggested, one eyebrow raised as he took in her shocked expression, his own face completely blank so that she had no idea what he was thinking. 'I can't make your wish come true if she doesn't want to.'

'But she will,' he butted in before Karen could open her mouth. 'She's helping the Wish people to send someone to Disneyland and I heard her say she'd do anything to help.'

'That's not quite the same thing,' Nathan began, but Matthew wasn't listening.

'Please, Dad. All you have to do is ask her. You'll see.' His big blue eyes were travelling agitatedly from one to the other and his voice was going higher and higher.

'Calm down, Matthew. Calm down,' Nathan soothed. 'That isn't the way to do it.'

'What, then?' he demanded suspiciously. His face was flushed and his breathing faster than it should be, but at least he wasn't working himself up any further. 'How *do* you do it?'

'Well. . .' Nathan paused, looking distinctly uncomfortable as he cast a sideways glance at Karen. 'When a man is going to ask a woman to marry him, he likes to take her out somewhere nice, perhaps to a restaurant for a meal.'

'Sort of buttering her up, like I do when I want something?' Matthew said shrewdly, and Karen had to swallow a laugh. It was such a strange feeling, standing by a hospital bed listening to a six-year-old boy trying to marry his father off to her. The whole situation felt surreal.

'Sort of,' Nathan agreed grimly, and she saw the tops of his ears turn red.

'So, why don't you try it?' Matthew said quietly, with a return to his strangely adult seriousness. 'She's a nice lady and she's good at looking after people.'

'I'll think about it,' Nathan said, falling back on the parent's perennial phrase.

'Dad! There isn't *time* to think about it.' The urgency was back in his voice. 'I had more blood tests done today.'

'All right,' Nathan conceded with a hand raised in

warning, and Karen was certain that the reminder about the tests had done more to change his mind than any consideration of his own loneliness. 'I agree to ask Karen to go out with me. . .'

'To butter her up?' he suggested hopefully.

'Exactly,' Nathan said wryly, his eyes raised to heaven. 'And then I'll let you know what she says.'

'She'll say yes,' Matthew said with utter conviction as he settled himself back against the pillows again. 'I know she will.'

'I'm sorry, Nathan; I had no idea that's what he had in mind.' Karen whirled to face him and began apologising as soon as they reached the office. 'I hope you don't think that I had anything to do with it. . .with putting the idea. . .' Karen bit her tongue before she used it to dig an even bigger hole to bury herself in.

'Don't worry,' he said drily as he sank into his usual chair. 'Matthew's quite capable of coming up with something like this without outside help. The only question is what are we going to do about it?'

'What do you mean?' Karen's hand froze as she reached for the jar of coffee, her emotions suddenly a frantic jumble of hopes and fears. 'What *can* we do about it?'

'Well, as far as Matthew's concerned, I need a wife to look after me and stop me feeling lonely when . . .*if* he dies.'

Karen glanced at him in grim acknowledgement of his slip of the tongue, but both of them knew that the first word was beginning to look more likely than the second.

'But you can't be contemplating getting married just

like that—just because your six-year-old son says you need to?'

'Why not, if he's got his heart set on it? You said yourself that I'd do anything to make him happy.'

'But . . .*marriage*?' An insidious excitement was beginning to build deep inside her as she listened to him speak. Did he really mean that he would be willing to marry her just to make his son happy? It was certainly beginning to sound like it.

And if they *were* to marry. . . He didn't know that she was already in love with him, but was there any chance that he would eventually come to love her in return?

'So, as long as Matthew doesn't know it's not a *real* marriage, he'll be happy,' she heard Nathan's husky voice concluding, and all her fragile dreams of happily ever after shattered about her.

'A mock marriage?' she said, driving the point home to herself in case she had any foolish ideas left. 'Just for Matthew's benefit?'

'It's the only solution, given the timespan we're talking about,' Nathan said with perfect logic. 'Do you agree?'

Matthew was ecstatic when they told him the news.

'I *knew* it!' he crowed. 'I *knew* if you asked her she'd say yes. That's why I talked to the church man.'

'Church man?' Nathan asked warily, glancing at Karen to see if she knew what he was talking about.

She shook her head and shrugged, but there was a nasty warning prickle between her shoulderblades.

'He's got a church in the hospital and he comes to talk to people,' Matthew explained kindly. 'So I talked to him.'

'And what did you talk about?'

'About the wedding, of course,' he said simply, as though it should have been obvious. 'I told him you needed to get married in a hurry and he said he can do it as soon as you like.'

Karen watched Nathan close his eyes tight as if he was hoping this was all a terrible nightmare that would disappear as soon as he opened them again.

She found herself holding her breath, not quite knowing which one of these two blue-eyed charmers she wanted to win this particular battle of wills.

'And when did you tell him to come back?' Nathan asked with more than a hint of sarcasm in his voice.

'At ten o'clock,' Matthew chirped, the tone of his father's words going straight over his head as he looked up at the clock at the end of the ward.

As though trapped in treacle, Karen swung her head to see the hands move round to ten as the ward door opened on Matthew's visitor.

'Do you, Nathan, take Karen to be your lawful wedded wife?' The solemn words rang out clearly over the hushed group gathered in the hospital chapel.

'I do,' the husky voice answered firmly.

'And do you, Karen, take Nathan to be your lawful wedded husband?'

'I do,' Karen echoed with barely a quiver in her voice, although the hand Nathan was holding was as cold as ice.

It had taken just three days to organise the wedding which was now taking place. Three days of alternating elation and blind panic as she wondered what on earth she was doing with her life.

She would never in a million years have believed

that two rational adults would allow themselves to be bulldozed into marriage by a six-year-old. . .

'Karen?'

Nathan's hands were gentle on her shoulders as he turned her towards him, and she realised when his head began to lower towards hers that the hospital chaplain had finished his closing words and Nathan was about to kiss her.

'May I?' he whispered softly, and she blinked, realising that some of her confusion must have shown on her face.

'Of course,' she replied, knowing that everyone was waiting for this traditional finale to the ceremony, and tilted her head to allow their lips to meet for a simple kiss.

Except she'd forgotten that with Nathan there was no such thing as a simple kiss.

In the blink of an eye she was engulfed by the memories and emotions of their one night of passion in Lapland and her brain ceased to function.

'My God,' Nathan gasped hoarsely when he rested his forehead against hers eons later. 'You make me forget where we are when you do that to me.'

'Me?' Karen squeaked in breathless embarrassment as she realised that there had been a whole chapel full of observers of that kiss, including a six-year-old boy gloating from the front pew. '*You're* the sex maniac— it says so on your coffee-mug!'

Nathan laughed softly and wrapped both arms around her in a gentle hug that spoke of respect and consideration and, for the first time, Karen dared to meet his beautiful sapphire eyes.

The whole world seemed to grow silent and their

smiles faded as they each seemed to search for something important. . .

'Until death us do part,' Nathan repeated for her ears alone, his voice utterly sincere, and Karen knew that everything was going to work out all right.

'Oh, Nathan, I do love you,' Karen said as the plane banked and made the final approach for Rovaniemi airport and she could see the snow falling.

'Uh-oh,' said a little voice by the window. 'Mushy stuff. Don't listen to it.'

Nathan had just leant towards her to steal a kiss but the boyish comment made him chuckle wryly instead.

'That's enough from you, my lad,' he cautioned. 'If you don't like it, you've only got yourself to blame. You're the one who picked her out for me.' He winked at Karen who wrinkled her nose at him in response.

This was a familiar refrain between her husband and their son, but a year ago she would never have believed that it would have turned out like this.

Her thoughts went back to the turmoil they'd gone through right from the first.

They'd hardly settled Matthew back in the ward after the brief ceremony in the hospital chapel than word had come through that the computer had come up with a possible match with a bone marrow donor.

It had seemed as if they waited years to find out whether the treatment had worked and it was in the euphoria of the first glowing report on the successful transplant that Nathan had picked her up and whirled her around while he finally admitted his love for her.

Now they were paying a return visit to the magical place where they had first realised that they had fallen in love, but this time it wasn't the trip of a lifetime for children nearing the end of their lives but for children with their whole lives in front of them.

'Will we be seeing Father Christmas today?' Matthew demanded as they waited for two children in wheelchairs to leave the plane first.

'I expect so, if you keep your eyes open,' Nathan said. His eyes followed Karen's gaze and he squeezed her hand as his thoughts mirrored hers. 'Just one year ago that was us,' he whispered. 'And look at us now.'

His deep blue eyes stroked her face as intimately as a touch and travelled on to the son they'd thought would be lost, before falling finally on the well-wrapped bundle she cradled in her arms.

'How's he doing?'

'He's warm and dry, well fed and getting very heavy,' she complained happily as she looked down on their new son with a besotted smile.

'We'll soon be at the hotel. Then you can put him down.'

'Unless we get delayed by elk on the road again,' she reminded him.

The transfer to the luxury coach went smoothly and in no time they were being escorted into one of the two-room cabins which were part of the same complex.

'Didn't you want to stay in the same cabin as last time and relive old memories?' she teased as Nathan carried in the last of the mountain of stuff the baby would need.

'No, thank you.' He glanced over his shoulder to make sure that Matthew was too busy exploring his own room to hear. 'This trip we won't be flouting Finnish sensibilities in a sauna because we'll have a bed to sleep in without an audience.' He tilted her chin up to capture her lips in a fleeting kiss. 'Now, let's get ourselves unpacked so that we can go across to eat.'

This time, Matthew was well enough to walk to the main cabin for the evening meal and was able to take part in the entertainment provided by the hotel, but they all knew that there was really only one reason why he had wanted to return to Lapland, and that would take place the next day.

'Come in. Come in,' a familiar accented voice called when they reached the little cabin deep in the woods and knocked at the door.

'Joulupukki!' Matthew greeted the red-suited figure as soon as he saw him. 'I've come back to show you something.'

The bright blue eyes narrowed as he looked at the smiling young man standing so tall and proud in front of him, one hand held out to show a much loved little reindeer.

'You gave me this when I came last year and told me that wishes can come true—and they do! Look!'

He beckoned towards Nathan who had been helping Karen out of the sleigh.

'Come on, Dad. Bring Mark in to see Father Christmas.'

As soon as he saw the well-wrapped bundle Karen was carrying, the old man hurried to welcome her into the cabin, closing the door to keep the heat in and offering her his own chair to sit in.

'And this is Mark?' he questioned gently, pulling the covers aside just far enough to see the sleeping face.

'He's my little brother,' Matthew announced proudly. 'I wished and wished that my dad would get married so he wouldn't be sad when I died, but then I got better and we had a family.'

'That is good.' The white head nodded. 'It is very good that such happiness should come from a wish.' He held his hand out to Nathan who gripped it warmly.

'And now, Matthew. What is it that brings you to see me this year? Do you have another wish for Christmas?'

'Oh, no!' His surprise was genuine. 'I don't need anything else. I just came back to say thank you.'

Karen saw the smile of pure pleasure which was shared by the young boy and the old man.

'You have done well with this boy,' he said quietly to Nathan and Karen when Matthew turned to look around at all the decorations in the little cabin. 'He has learned what many never do—that it is the *people* who matter when you make a wish for Christmas.'

Nathan's arm circled Karen's shoulders and she looked up at him with love in her smile. She knew that between them they had everything they could wish for.

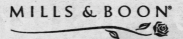

MILLS & BOON®

Medical Romance™

Books for enjoyment this month...

RESPONDING TO TREATMENT — Abigail Gordon
BRIDAL REMEDY — Marion Lennox
A WISH FOR CHRISTMAS — Josie Metcalfe
WINGS OF DUTY — Meredith Webber

Treats in store!

Watch next month for these absorbing stories...

TAKE A CHANCE ON LOVE — Jean Evans
PARTNERS IN LOVE — Maggie Kingsley
DRASTIC MEASURES — Laura MacDonald
PERFECT PARTNERS — Carol Wood

GET 4 BOOKS
AND A MYSTERY GIFT

FREE

Return this coupon and we'll send you 4 Medical Romance™ novels and a mystery gift absolutely FREE! We'll even pay the postage and packing for you.

We're making you this offer to introduce you to the benefits of Reader Service: FREE home delivery of brand-new Medical Romance novels, at least a month before they are available in the shops, FREE gifts and a monthly Newsletter packed with information.

Accepting these FREE books and gift places you under no obligation to buy, you may cancel at any time, even after receiving just your free shipment. Simply complete the coupon below and send it to:

MILLS & BOON® READER SERVICE, FREEPOST, CROYDON, SURREY, CR9 3WZ.

No stamp needed

Yes, please send me 4 free Medical Romance novels and a mystery gift. I understand that unless you hear from me, I will receive 4 superb new titles every month for just £2.10* each, postage and packing free. I am under no obligation to purchase any books and I may cancel or suspend my subscription at any time, but the free books and gift will be mine to keep in any case. (I am over 18 years of age)

M6LE

Ms/Mrs/Miss/Mr _____

Address _____

_____

_____ Postcode _____